CW00672954

DEFYING THE ALPHA

EMILIA ROSE

Cover Designer: Covers by Christian

Editing by: Jovana Shirley, Unforeseen Editing, www.unforeseenediting.com

Proofreading by: Heart Full of Reads

Beta reading by: Alice Nicole, Angel Wakefield, Brittany Pugh, Joanne Procter, Kayla Lutz, Leshae Scheepers

Emilia Rose

emiliarosewriting@gmail.com

ISBN: 978-1-954597-03-7

This book is dedicated to Carnegie Coffee Company for letting me sit in their shop, drinking loads of jasmine green tea while editing this book, for five hours a day for two weeks straight.

CHAPTER 1

ISABELLA

"*I'm stressed the fuck out, Isabella,*" Roman said through our personal mind link. His voice was tense, gruff, and filled with all of our worries from the past few weeks, ever since I'd become leader of the Lycans.

I shimmied up to our bed's headboard, stared at the twinkling moonflowers that I had decorated our windowsill with, and drew a finger up the center of my bare thigh. *"Come home,"* I said through the link. *"I know what will calm you down."*

After letting out a low and sensual growl, Roman told me he'd be home soon and cut off the mind link. I parted my thighs and stuck my hand between my legs, toying with what Roman used to play with every night.

Something had been off with him lately. Maybe it was the constant stress and separation that my duties with the Lycans caused. Ryker had left me with so many broken, smashed, and crushed ties with alphas who had once trusted us warriors.

People were angry. Wolves refused to ask for our help with rogues. Unsettled and outspoken wolves and packs stirred up trouble deeper into the forest. And of course, I had to be the one to try to mend the wounds, the broken trust, and the heartbreak of losing loved ones to rogues—just because Ryker had wanted power.

After taking a deep breath of the crisp midnight air, I slipped a hand into my underwear and rubbed small circles around my clit, clenching. I needed Roman inside of me to make those worries disappear just for a few moments as he made sweet love to me … or fucked me roughly—I didn't *really* have a preference.

All I wanted was to grip on to each ridge of his long, thick cock, to feel him pumping into me in a steady rhythm, for him to wrap his hand around my throat as he whispered into my ear with that filthy mouth of his.

Tilting my head to look out the window, I found his golden eyes staring at me from the forest. I clenched and curled my toes. Goddess, he never got tired of watching me play with myself for him.

He loved every second of it.

Rubbing myself even faster, I spread my legs and let him eye me. He was probably hard, rubbing one out in the forest before he came up to our bedroom to destroy me, wondering how good I'd feel after a couple of weeks of holding back.

The moonflowers glowed even brighter on my windowsill, twinkling under the moonlight itself and lighting up the dark room around me. I breathed them in once more, a tinge of an unfamiliar scent filling my nostrils.

I tensed slightly at the scent, my wolf purring. But too many things were on my mind tonight, especially the meeting with the alphas tomorrow. This entire week, my wolf had been on edge, as we thought something was bound to go wrong at the gathering. Something always did. So, I decided to ignore it, just for tonight.

After closing my eyes for a moment, I sank into the sheets. The front door opened, and a wave of pleasure rushed through me. Roman was here, coming to take me for the first time in days.

With every step he took up the stairs, I clenched harder.

Calm down, Isabella. He's our mate. We may not get many intimate nights together anymore, but we see him every day.

But even I couldn't quite calm myself down because seeing him was the best part of my day by far.

When the bedroom door opened, I drew my knees together and smiled up at Roman. He stood at the door, brown hair ruffled in a wild, savage mess, hazel eyes with streaks of damaging gold, huge muscles flexed against his salmon-colored button-up.

"Isabella," he murmured, voice lower and gruffer than it'd sounded in the mind link.

One by one, he unbuttoned his shirt and let it hang off his shoulders. That golden gaze traveled down and back up my body, canines emerging from under his lips. "My dear Isabella."

I rolled onto my stomach, crawled over to the edge of the bed, and crooked a finger in his direction. "I'm not waiting for you any longer," I said, looping my fingers in his belt loops and tugging him closer. My hand slipped into his pants.

He grasped my jaw and forced me to stare up into his intense eyes. "Not yet." He stepped toward me, letting the front of his pants brush against my breasts, which were covered in his favorite lacy black bra. "I'm going to enjoy you first."

Grabbing my legs, he pulled my to the edge of the bed

until my ass hung off it and then trailed one finger from my chin down the center of my chest to my underwear. His lips moved from one side of my neck to the other. When he reached my mark, he nibbled on it and sucked the scars from his immense canines into his mouth.

Fingers rubbing against my clit, he continued to kiss down my chest, marking it up with red little hickeys that I loved to peek at whenever I was having a bad day. He hooked his teeth inside my bra cup and gently pulled up on it.

"Take this off," he ordered.

I unclipped my bra and let the straps fall down my arms, my breasts dropping out of it. After growling lowly, he latched his teeth around my nipple and sucked hard on it.

"I've been waiting all week to fuck you."

He kissed down to my underwear, hooked his fingers around the waistband, and pulled them down my legs.

I spit on my fingers and brushed them against my bare clit, just aching to be touched. We had both been so busy and so tired to be this intimate for a long time, but not tonight. Tonight I needed him.

After grasping my hand, he pinned it to the bed. "Mine," he said against my folds, his breath warming my core. "It's *mine* to touch." He pressed his lips on the top of my mound and slowly worked his way down to my clit, teasing it with his tongue.

When he ran a finger down my slit and pushed it into my aching pussy, I clenched around him and whimpered. I moved my hips from side to side, trying to relieve the tension building in my core, and thrust my fingers into his hair. "Roman," I breathed.

"So tight for me," he murmured against me.

He rested my legs on his shoulders and pressed his lips to my cunt, eyes closing as if this was the most pleasurable thing to him. His fingers moved faster in and out of me. I curled my fingers around strands of his brown hair and tugged him closer to me.

Oh Moon Goddess, what had I done to deserve a man like this?

My legs tingled when he drew his mouth and nose up my inner thigh. He stood, pushed down his pants, and took his hard cock in his hand, slapping it against my sopping pussy. As he pushed it inside of me, my pussy tightened around him.

"Fuck, Isabella. Wrap your arms around me."

He grabbed my legs and lifted me off of the bed, thrusting into me hard. I gripped on to his back for dear life and gazed over his shoulder and out the window.

Our flowers blinked and twinkled on the windowsill. That unfamiliar scent drifted through my nostrils again. Roman continued to pump into me, each thrust sending me closer and closer to him and to the brink of orgasm. My breasts bounced against his chest, and he took one in his hand and sucked my nipple into his mouth, biting down lightly.

I furrowed my brows, my lips parting in delight, and moaned into his ear. Wave after wave of ecstasy pumped through me. In a complete daze, my gaze drifted from the flowers to the forest.

Hazel eyes stared in our direction.

My entire body tensed, and I dug my nails into Roman's back.

Someone was watching us. Someone I didn't recognize.

"Roman." I tried pulling away from him slightly to get a better view of the wolf in the woods. Nobody had hazel eyes with golden streaks in them like that.

Roman thrust harder into me, and the wolf continued to stare at us.

"Roman … stop."

Tossing me onto the bed, he flipped me around and

pushed my chest against the mattress. "Stop?" he asked, tugging on my hair to pull me closer. The air was filled with his mint scent and the thick tension between us. "I've been waiting all fucking week to be inside of your tight pussy, feel you clench around me, listen to you whimper." He smirked against his mark. "I'm not stopping now."

I clutched on to the bedsheets. I didn't want to stop either.

Maybe I was just seeing things. Maybe I was just ...

After glancing back out the window, we locked eyes. Under the flickering moonflowers in the forest, I swore the wolf smirked. Fucking smirked at me like he was taunting me and taunting Roman.

When he walked out into the moonlight, I tensed. He was incredibly huge—almost alpha-rank big—with white fur and sparkling hazel eyes.

Instead of looking away, I turned my upper body toward Roman and pushed on his chest. "There's someone watching us."

Roman looked out the window at the wolf and then back at me, lips curling into a smirk. "Watching how an alpha fucks his mate to sleep," Roman said arrogantly. He crawled onto the bed between my legs and kissed my neck, sucking on his mark. "Relax, Isabella. Don't let him ruin our night."

"You're okay with this?" I asked breathlessly, arching my back as he kissed lower. I glanced out the window to see the unfamiliar wolf still staring at us, watching with so much intent.

Roman thrust his fingers into my pussy, getting them wet with my juices. "You are." He pulled his fingers out of me and drew them down the center of my body, between my breasts. "You're soaked for me, baby." He stuffed his fingers into my mouth. "Does being watched turn on, my dear Isabella?"

Clenching, I stared up into my mate's golden eyes and swallowed. "I … I …"

Roman kissed me on the jaw, letting his lips linger. "You don't have to say it. Just turn around for me and get on all fours, so he can watch me finish what I have been craving all week."

My heart raced in my chest. Though I never expected this to be one of Roman's kinks, I turned around and knelt on the bed on all fours, arching my back and letting my breasts swing gently as Roman grasped my waist.

"Good girl," Roman said, grabbing a handful of my hair in one hand and my ass in the other. He thrust into me from behind, filling me completely. "You're being such a good girl for me today, not a brat, like usual."

I tightened around him and moaned, loving his praise. My fingers curled into the bedsheets, and I took another glimpse at the wolf in the woods. Something about Roman wanting someone else to watch hadn't felt right to me at first, but he had watched me countless nights. Why had I expected him *not* to like something like this?

This was an erotic display of dominance.

And my Roman was nothing but a hard, dominant mate.

"Have I finally fucked that bratty mouth enough to make you obedient?" Roman asked, pounding into me from behind.

A low growl escaped my throat, my canines lengthening. "No matter how rough you are with me, I'll never obey you. You should know that, you—"

He pushed my head against the mattress, posted one foot on the bed to fuck me even harder, and slipped an arm around my waist to smacked me on my aching clit. "I won't be able to break you? Is that what you think?" Roman asked, slapping me there again.

I yelped out, my pussy tightening around his cock.

Tugging me up by the hair until my back was pressed against his taut chest, Roman growled into my ear, "Let's get one thing straight, Isabella. Look out the fucking window, open that pretty little mouth of yours, and scream my name, or neither of us will come tonight. And I know that this tight, aching little pussy"—he slapped my clit again—"is just waiting to swallow my cum."

Squeezing my eyes closed, I shook my head at him. So close … I was so close to coming all over his cock without his permission, so close to letting him really punish me in front of this man for disobeying the big, bad alpha.

After snaking a hand around my neck, he slapped my clit hard. "Do it."

"No."

"Now, Isabella."

"No …" I whimpered.

He slammed himself into me, hitting my cervix and making me scream. I opened my eyes to stare out the window at the wolf.

"Roman!" I yelled, toes curling. "Roman, please, give it to me."

Roman sank himself deep into me, stilled, and groaned into my ear. I relaxed into his arms, watching the wolf pad back into the forest and disappear into the night.

After Roman pulled out of me, I turned around and collapsed onto the bed. "We need to talk, Alpha."

CHAPTER 2

ROMAN

*I*sabella's moonflowers flickered on the windowsill, lighting up the room. I shut off the lights and crawled into bed with her, listening to pack members howl on their midnight runs.

"What was that?" Isabella asked, pulling the blankets over our naked bodies.

I brushed some hair out of her face. "What was what?"

She rolled her bright blue eyes. "You know exactly what I'm talking about. Did you ask that wolf to come and watch?" she asked, gnawing on her lip. "Because everyone in our pack knows not to come here, especially this late at night *to watch* us."

There wasn't anything I could get past Isabella.

My lips curled into a small smile. "He's a beta in a nearby pack, someone I used to train with. I asked him to come. Did you enjoy it?"

Cheeks flushed, she looked down at my chest and gave the slightest nod. "I just never thought you'd like that."

I turned onto my back and stared up at the ceiling. There were many things Isabella didn't know about me yet even though we were mates and once good friends. So much had changed between us once my father started training me to be alpha.

"I enjoy it," I said.

"Have you done it before?" she asked me.

"Yes," I said hesitantly, all the bad memories coming back.

She widened her eyes and sat up. "Really?" she asked, actually curious. "With who?"

"I don't think you really want to know, Isabella. It's in the past," I said, yet she continued to stare down at me with those big eyes. I sighed and pulled her down with me, holding her in my arms. "My ex–best friend and my ex-girlfriend."

Somehow, her eyes got even wider. "With that Scarlett girl?" Isabella asked, scrunching her nose in disgust. "I only heard rumors about her, but I hated her with my entire being because she took you away from me." She paused, the moon-flowers glowing off her eyes. "Who was your friend?"

I shook my head.

"His name is Kylo. Kylo Marks."

"Kylo of the Moon Ridge Pack?" she asked with wide eyes. "What happened between you two?"

I clenched my jaw, thinking back to my mother and my father, back to Scarlett, back to the days I'd vowed to kill Kylo if I ever saw him on my property. That man had had it out for me for over four years now, and tomorrow would be the first day I'd see him in years.

"A falling-out," I said, refusing to go into any more detail than that now.

Isabella sat up in bed again, shaking her head. "Kylo has been one of the most outspoken alphas after the world found out that Ryker had betrayed the Lycans. He'll be at the meeting tomorrow." She curled her knees to her chest and chewed on the inside of her cheek. "I'm nervous that I won't be able to settle the alpha down."

Trailing my fingers across her hip, I sat up and placed my lips on her mark. "Don't be nervous, my dear Isabella," I said, feeling her relax under my lips. "Kylo won't be a problem for you. I'll take care of him. What we should be nervous about is the unrest between some of the warring packs."

"Unrest?" she whispered.

"Cayden told me earlier that wolves have been more feral than usual lately," I said, tucking some hair behind her ear. "And I don't want you to get roped into it and willingly put yourself in more danger."

"I'm the leader of the Lycans, Roman. Danger comes with the job."

"And you're my mate. Protecting you comes with mine."

CHAPTER 3

ISABELLA

*L*oud, irate chatter spilled out into the hallway from the Lycans' auditorium. I bounced on my toes and held my hands to my stomach, feeling the need to puke. Alphas, mates, and warriors from all packs were here, worried about what would happen now that Ryker had both betrayed them and died by his own mate's hands.

Trust in the Lycans was dwindling faster than I'd expected.

Roman had been right about one thing last night: uneasy energy had fallen over our forest between warring packs. If I couldn't get across today that they could count on us to protect them, I feared war against us would follow... or maybe something much worse.

"Izzy!" Vanessa said. She placed her purple-manicured fingers on my arms from behind and leaned over my shoulder, strands of her blonde hair falling into her face. "Calm down, girl."

While Vanessa and I hadn't been the best of friends, we had grown closer the past few weeks. She finally respected the boundaries I'd set for her with Roman and had quickly risen to become one of the strongest warriors in Roman's pack.

"Is everyone here?" I asked her, peeking into the cramped auditorium.

She opened the door wider for me, trying to usher me in, but my feet wouldn't move a damn inch. I hated public speaking more than I'd hated Vanessa in high school. Everything that happened today would affect the Lycans and how people viewed them in the coming months.

"Yes," Vanessa said. "Raj, Roman, all the other alphas. You'll do great. Now, get in there." She pushed me into the room and closed the door, letting it clatter behind us.

A sudden silence engulfed the room as alphas stared at me.

Vanessa whispered, "Good luck," to me and sat in the front row, next to Roman, who gave me one of those supportive smiles.

I walked to the front with my heart racing in my chest and my wolf suddenly on full alert. There was an unfamiliar, *almost*-soothing scent somewhere in the auditorium that she couldn't quite place.

Before I made it to the podium, alphas started whispering to their lunas and betas about me—an eighteen-year-old woman leading the Lycans.

I swallowed hard and shifted uncomfortably, grasping the edges of the stand. "Good morning," I said.

A couple people grunted in response, but the majority of the crowd was silent. Moon Goddess, this was not even starting well; I couldn't see it ending any better. Glancing around the room, I locked eyes with a man toward the center of the room.

Gold eyes. Blazing, intense, smoldering gold eyes.

With light-brown hair parted to the side, a chiseled jaw with a five o'clock shadow, and muscles so taut that they nearly ripped through his white button-up, the alpha stared me down like I was some sort of prey that he wanted to devour.

The entire time I spoke to the men and women, he stared and stared and stared. My wolf gazed back at him, realizing that the unfamiliar pine scent she'd smelled earlier was radiating off him in waves.

Something about him screamed danger, hazard, threat.

I clenched my jaw, turned away from him for the first time this morning, and continued speaking to the alphas, "And that's why you need—"

"Excuse me, Isabella," the man with gold eyes said, standing up and commanding attention so naturally.

It doesn't intimidate me, I told myself. *It doesn't. Not at all.*

A man so wickedly handsome couldn't intimidate me.

Roman looked over his shoulder, clenched his jaw, and rolled his eyes.

"Yes, Alpha …"

"Kylo," the man said. "Alpha Kylo Marks of the Moon-Ridge Pack."

Almost immediately, I pressed my lips together and sucked in a quiet breath. This was Kylo Marks, ex–best friend of Roman and the most outspoken alpha against the trustworthiness of the Lycans.

A fiery hatred appeared in Roman's eyes. While he had told me last night that he hated Kylo for the rumors spreading like wildfire—that he wanted to seize control of Roman's pack—there was something deeper between them that had happened. I could just sense it.

"Isn't it true that you went behind Alpha Roman's back to join the Lycans?" Kylo asked.

I clenched my teeth together and balled my hands into fists behind the podium. "We are not here to discuss me or my acceptance into the Lycans, Alpha Kylo," I said, keeping calm. "We are here to discuss the relationship between the Lycans and the packs."

Lips curling into an even more frightening smirk, he nodded. "And that's exactly what I plan to do." Turning toward the group of alphas, he held his arms out like he was a king talking to his subjects. "Who says that she wouldn't abandon the alliances she's proposing for her own self-interest when the time came?" He shifted back to me. "I mean, you did leave your own mate to join a group of criminals."

Roman growled through his canines, "Sit down, Kylo."

Breathe, Isabella. Don't freak out on him.

"The Lycans are not a group of criminals. We protect packs from rogues, so alphas like you can lead their packs without problem and without added stress."

He furrowed his dark, thick brows at me. "Your leader was *ordering* rogues to kill alphas."

Something about him got under my skin, made my blood boil with so much anger.

"He is not our leader, Kylo. I am," I said, pushing my shoulders back.

"*Alpha* Kylo," he corrected. Again, he looked around the room. "Can we really trust someone like this? Someone who was under Ryker's influence? Someone who lied to her own mate for her own selfish reasons? If she goes behind her mate's back, she will go behind ours."

Because I was getting nowhere with him and because Roman looked like he was about to rip Kylo's head off, I stared Kylo down. "Let's break, so some of us can cool down."

Kylo curled the corner of his lip up slightly, taunting me. "Does the princess need a break?"

This time, Raj growled from the front, standing up and preparing to fight. I held my hand up to command him to back down and pressed my lips together.

"I am a luna and the leader of the Lycans. I will not be disrespected, Kylo. I want nothing but peace between the Lycans and the other packs. Calm down during the break or leave."

After turning off the microphone, I stepped down from the stage and walked out of the auditorium. As soon as I made it to the hallway, I plastered my back against the wall as I took a breath of fresh, untainted air and closed my eyes.

Moon Goddess, help me. How was I going to convince them to trust me when Kylo had it out for me for some ungodly reason? And why the hell was my wolf so anxious, just *looking* at him? He wasn't my mate. She should never feel this way about him.

"Damn him," I said to Raj when he exited the auditorium.

We walked down the hallway together, passing the refreshments room and other Lycans, who I'd told to do some damage control.

"Find me as much information on Kylo Marks as you can get. I need it all. He's not going to stop me from having peace with the other alphas."

Raj nodded and hurried down the hallway toward his office. Instead of locking myself away in my office, I decided on some much-needed sunlight, something to help me think clearly because, now, I was blind with rage and ...

Lust, my wolf said in my mind.

No, I was not blind with lust. No fucking way.

I turned the corner and bumped right into the asshole himself, Kylo.

"Isabella."

"Kylo," I said, straightening my back. "What do you want?"

"So defensive." He clicked his tongue at me and shook his head. "It's quite sexy on you."

I sneered at him. "I have a mate," I said through clenched teeth.

"I had a mate once too," Kylo said, stepping toward me.

I didn't like the closeness between us. It made my wolf too anxious to be still and quiet for just a moment.

"And your dear, precious Roman took her from me. Wouldn't it make you angry if that same woman was trying to get with Roman again, take him away from you?"

"You're lying." I tilted my head and stepped closer to him, staring up into his big, beautifully agonizing brown eyes. "You're trying to get under my skin, trying to split us apart, so that we're weak."

"You don't have to believe me, princess. I just thought I'd tell you before he breaks your cold little heart," he said, brushing his fingers up my forearm. "A strong woman like you deserves to know."

"What do you want?" I asked again.

He isn't getting to me. He isn't getting to me. He isn't getting to me.

So much mischief lay in those golden-streaked brown eyes. He thought that he had power over me, that he was the one with control. But he had no control over me and *definitely* none over my wolf either.

"I want you to back off and disassemble the Lycans." He stepped closer to me, nearly pinning me against the wall, and brushed his fingers against my hip. "Maybe I want to make sure you don't get screwed by Roman too." He leaned down slightly, so his lips brushed against my ear. "*Take you for myself.*"

I snaked a hand around his neck, squeezed tightly, and twirled us around, so I was pinning him to the wall. "Don't you dare speak to me like that. I'm not someone you can push around. I'm the leader of the Lycans, a wolf that could kill you, if I wanted."

"A dominant woman." Kylo hummed, drawing his fingers up my forearm. "I've always wondered what it'd be like to be with one. To have her pin me to the wall, press her body against mine …" He leaned down further, nose grazing against my ear. "To have her think that I couldn't break her just by brushing my fingers—"

I squeezed his neck a bit harder. Moon Goddess, he was getting on my nerves.

"Stop it," I said, my heart racing.

"Why? Is it turning you on?" he asked playfully. I growled, and he chuckled. "It is."

"Listen to me and listen closely, Kylo. You can try to break the peace between the Lycans and the packs, but if you even *try* to come between Roman and me, I will rip you into tiny little pieces and feed you to the rogues myself."

He shoved me against the opposite wall so easily, his strength overpowering mine. "You can think that, princess." He drew a finger up the column of my neck to my chin, forcing me to look up at him. "But when you find him and Scarlett in the refreshments room, alone, you won't want to kill me. It'll be him you want to destroy."

I gripped his wrist and dug my claws into it until I drew blood. He didn't know shit about where Roman was.

"I'm the only person who can help you reach your full potential. Unlike Roman, I'm not afraid of a woman like you, one who's strong, hardheaded, one who likes to go after what she wants. I don't get jealous of a powerful woman and leader."

My wolf was oddly quiet, and I hated it. I pushed him away from me, my fingers tingling.

Kylo smirked and stepped away from me. "If you want to settle for an average life, you can stay with Roman, who will never give you the control your bratty self so desires in and out of the bedroom."

"Fuck you," I said.

He leaned close once more. "Maybe you can once you get rid of your lousy mate," he said. "But for now, just know that I'm coming for you, princess."

CHAPTER 4

ROMAN

*A*lone in the refreshments room, I took a long sip of a beer and blew out a deep breath. Holy fuck, this meeting was not going how Isabella had wanted it to. Just as she'd started to convince some alphas to trust her again, Kylo had stood and fucked it all up.

After this meeting was over, I planned to *politely* talk to Kylo alone and tell him to fuck off. Isabella could try talking to him and convince him to shut his mouth, but she didn't know Kylo like I did. He was a prick, just like his father. And I'd take care of him as my father had taken care of his.

"All by your lonesome?" someone said from behind me.

I cringed at the sound of Scarlett's tacky voice and turned around to see her standing in the doorway, dressed in the tightest damn dress she could squeeze herself into. She sauntered into the room, dark brown hair in soft curls down her shoulders.

"You look so much better than the last time I saw you, Romie. Really filled out."

Rolling my eyes, I placed my drink down and started for the door.

She jumped in my way and pressed her hands against my chest. "Oh, come on. Don't be like that. I just want to talk." She twirled around with a big, stupid grin on her face, like she thought this was some sort of game. "See anything different about me?"

"No. Now, move."

She leaned forward and pressed her breasts together. "Oh, come on, Romie. Just guess then."

After coming to the conclusion that I wouldn't get out of here without force, I rocked back on my heels and gave her the most uninterested expression I could muster. "You let your hair grow?"

"Guess again."

Moon Goddess, fucking help me.

"You lost some weight."

"Getting closer," she said, twirling around even slower this time.

I shook my head. "I don't fucking know, Scarlett. I'm not in the mood for you either."

She drew her hands up her hips, accentuating her curves. "Well, I know you're an ass guy, so I started working out for you. I think it's been paying off." She turned around to show me her ass and gazed back at me with huge, desperate fuck-me eyes. "Oh, come on. Don't pretend like you didn't notice." She snickered. "Tell me, Roman, does Isabella please you the way I used to with Kylo?"

Fuck being nice to her anymore.

I stepped toward her and curled my hand around her throat, which was a mistake.

"You don't have to say it. I didn't think she could. I know

what you need and what you want—obedience. A strong warrior like her could never give you that. Has too much other shit on her mind. Me …" She smiled, eyes lighting up with excitement. "If I were yours, I'd be sitting on my knees, waiting for you by your bed every single night. I'd make you the man of your pack."

I squeezed hard until her face turned blue and pulled her closer. "Isabella pleases me more than you ever could, pup," I said into her ear. "Next time you mention her or Kylo, I won't hesitate to snap your fragile, worthless neck. Do you understand me, Scarlett?"

She brushed her fingers against my abdomen and made me tense.

"Do you understand?" I repeated.

"One day, Roman," she threatened, ripping herself out of my grip. "One day, you're going to wish you'd chosen differently, wish you'd chosen *me*, because there is a darkness coming, and neither you nor Isabella will be able to stop it." She walked to the door, staring me down. "You'll crumble, and I'm the only one who'll be able to save you."

Narrowing my eyes at her, I blew another annoyed breath out of my nose. *Darkness?* Did she think she was some kind of prescience? What kind of weird shit had she been on these past four years?

When she turned to walk out of the room, she stopped at the door. "Oh, hi, Isabella. It's nice to finally meet you." She threw me a wicked grin and left.

Isabella stepped into the doorway with her arms crossed over her chest and her eyes wide with fear. "That was Scarlett, wasn't it?" she asked.

I stepped toward her, but she stepped back. My wolf howled inside me at her blatant rejection to be close.

"Why were you talking to her in here, alone?"

Anger rushed through me at the mere thought of Scarlett

trapping me in here, alone, just to piss off Isabella and get her not to trust me. While I knew that Kylo and Scarlett had split up for years, they could be working together again, trying to tear me down.

"Answer me, Roman. Why were you in here with Scarlett, your ex-girlfriend?"

"She wanted to talk," I told her, not knowing what else to say.

I didn't want to tell Isabella that Scarlett had come on to me because I didn't want her getting jealous. We had less than two minutes before the meeting resumed. She needed to be thinking clearly.

After pressing her lips together, she shook her head. "Kylo was right," she whispered to herself, grabbing my half-empty beer from the counter and taking a swig. She looked at her watch. "We have to get back to the fucking meeting."

"Kylo?" I asked, following her out of the room. I hated—fucking loathed—that he had been alone with her for even just a second. I *never* wanted that man to look at, think about, or even be close to my mate. "You talked to him?"

She stepped into the auditorium. "Yes."

Before she could get any farther, I snatched her wrist and pulled her back toward me. "And?"

"And he said that Scarlett was trying to take you away from me."

She looked toward Scarlett, who sat on the opposite side of the auditorium with the rest of the warriors in her pack. They all had vicious, bloodthirsty looks on their faces today, which was unusual for a fairly peaceful pack.

Tugging her closer, I stared down into her eyes. "You know I would never jeopardize us. You're my mate, who I've waited years for." I brushed some strands of hair from her face, tucking them behind her ear. "You're mine, Isabella. Mine."

Kylo stared at us from his seat and had the damn audacity to smirk at me and wiggle his fingers in an attempt to fuck with me. I curled my claws into Isabella's hip. That mischievous look in his eye told me one thing: he wanted to break me by using Isabella—whether that meant telling her lies or *killing* her.

She was one of my greatest weaknesses, just like Scarlett had been his years ago.

And Kylo wanted payback, sweet and sinful payback.

CHAPTER 5

KYLO

*D*ressed in navy pants that clung to her ass and a white blouse with just enough buttons undone to show off her breasts, Isabella squirmed in front of the podium as she finished up the meeting, bright blue eyes flickering to mine every other moment.

I intently listened to her stumble over her words, watched her cheeks flush pink, and felt her uneasiness permeate the air. It should've made me gloat in glory that I, Kylo Marks, had accomplished what I had come to do. But her nerves were giving me anxiety, and that anxiety was riling up my wolf.

Help her, my wolf pleaded with me. *You made her nervous.*

Ignoring his comments, I continued to listen to her spiel about the Lycans. While they seemed like decent people, ever since Ryker had betrayed the alphas and been executed for his crimes, a darkness had been unleashed onto the forest.

Now wasn't the time to reunite the Lycans and the packs,

as the Lycans couldn't do shit with inter- and intra-pack conflict, especially not this kind. It was a sort of chaos that I had never seen in my twenty-two years of life.

They had eliminated most of the rogues, which was the point of their little team.

We didn't need them now.

Settle her down, my wolf continued, watching her rub her reddening neck.

I rolled my eyes. *No,* I said back to him.

"Do you find the need for peace annoying, Kylo?" Isabella asked, stopping mid-stage to blink expectantly at me. She placed her hand on her waist, accentuating her curves, and I could do nothing, except suck in a sharp breath.

Now! my wolf said. *This is our chance to talk to her wolf.*

Curling my lip up in disgust at the thoughts racing through my wolf's mind, I shook my head. "No, carry on. I just don't see the point in this. The damage Ryker caused has been done and cannot be taken back."

She pressed her lips together, cheeks flushing red, and turned back to the group.

As Isabella teetered back and forth, I glanced over at Roman, who sat in the front of the auditorium, showing me his teeth for capturing his mate's attention. He probably thought I was going to rip his mate out of his life, just as he had ripped Scarlett out of mine years ago.

Maybe. I hadn't decided what I'd do with Isabella yet.

Neither had my wolf, apparently. He couldn't seem to stop staring.

CHAPTER 6

ISABELLA

*A*fter stepping out of the stuffy auditorium, I ran my hands through my hair and cursed Kylo out under my breath. Thanks to that stupid asshole, I had made no progress in trying to convince the alphas to trust the Lycans. Between him *and* Scarlett's pack, who was stirring up chaos, this meeting might've made everything worse.

Warriors were questioning our abilities, alphas were questioning our trust, and I was questioning how I could get myself out of this mess. I rested my back against the wall, shoulders slumped forward in defeat.

"Prepare for war, princess," Kylo said, walking through the doors and down the hallway.

I clenched my hands into fists, watching him walk away. It wasn't an empty threat. According to Roman, Kylo had been lusting over his territory for a long time. Now that nobody trusted me, he had others on his side to join him in battle and aid him in victory.

Worse than that, my damn wolf wouldn't stop staring at him. I tore my gaze away from his huge back muscles flexing through his button-up shirt and clenched my jaw. What the hell was wrong with her? She was acting almost as interested in him as she did with Roman.

My wolf was beginning to aggravate me.

Kylo had some goddamn nerve.

Raj cleared his throat and handed me a file filled with freshly printed papers. "Kylo," he said, stuffing his hands into his pockets. We stepped farther away from the auditorium entrance, so nobody would listen in. "Alpha Kylo. He's from one of the strongest packs in the whole region, quickly fighting his way to the top and making a name for himself."

I opened the file, skimmed through the information, and tried to gather my own thoughts about that man because my wolf was being awfully quiet again, and it didn't sit right with me.

"He is an incredible warrior, inherited the title of alpha from his brother who'd died in battle, is currently mateless, as he rejected his previous mate"—my wolf purred—"was born under the Wolf Moon, had a—"

I furrowed my brows. "Born under the Wolf Moon?"

I had been born under the Wolf Moon.

Besides the Blood Moon, the Wolf Moon was the rarest moon to be born under. While it happened once a year on the same day, the wolves who survived their birth under such a moon were the strongest. Some even said they were given powers to protect by the Moon Goddess herself. A couple wolves had even outranked alphas.

An alpha who was also a Wolf Moon baby would be incredibly powerful, could command rooms of people who didn't even know him, and could rip people apart at the snap of his fingers.

Raj nodded. "Yes. You know that wolves born during the

Wolf Moon are some of the strongest. Their strength is similar to that of the original werewolves and possess powers close to that of the Moon Goddess."

Was that why I felt connected to him? We had been born under the same moon. I blew a breath out of my nose. Of course, that was the reason my wolf was so anxious around him.

Raj gazed down the hallway at his mate, Jane. "I'll find more information on him."

"No. That's all I needed to know. But, Raj, prepare the Lycans. Kylo is unnerving and confident. I don't want to be caught off guard, especially after how he acted today in the meeting." And in the hallway earlier.

When Raj disappeared out the side doors with Jane, I hurried down the hall to my office, flipping through the file to read about Kylo. Immersed in newspaper snippets and articles about him, I jumped when someone thrust me right against the door outside my office.

"Where do you think you're going?" Roman murmured into my ear. "Sneaking back into your office before I had a chance to touch"—he slipped his hand under the waistband of my pants—"this." He drew his nose up the column of my neck and brushed it against his mark. "It's almost as if you want me to punish you, my dear Isabella."

"Punish me?" I asked with feigned surprise. I drew my knees together, loving the feel of his cock hardening against my ass. "Never."

After snaking his other hand up my neck, he pulled me closer. "Every single day of your fucking life, you want me to punish you, Isabella. You can't resist it." He brushed his fingers across my underwear and right above my clit, rubbing my wetness. "You're already so wet, just thinking about it."

I turned my head to the side to look up at him. "Maybe I'd

29

be a good girl if you actually punished me instead of making empty little promises. I want an alpha who knows how to really give it to me well."

"You don't like my punishments?" he growled into my ear.

"No." Lie.

He trailed a finger down my folds, pressing it against my entrance but never into me. "I'm going to make you love them," he said, voice gruff and filled with tainted spite. He sank his teeth into his mark and sucked on it harshly, making me moan. After placing his entire hand over my mouth, he said, "Shh, shh, shh, Isabella. Everyone is still here. You don't want them to hear you, do you?"

I squeezed my eyes shut, my pussy pulsing and desperately waiting for him to be inside of me. Moon Goddess, this was going to be rough. I could already feel it.

Roman grasped my breast through my shirt and seized my nipple, tugging on it harder than he ever had before. I shook my head, pain shooting through me.

"You might not want anyone to hear you," Roman said, rubbing my clit with his thumb as his fingers still poked against my entrance. "But I do. Now, beg."

My toes curled. "No."

After I blatantly defied him, he growled into my ear, crept his hand up under my shirt, and yanked down my bra cups, so he could see my nipples press through my thin shirt. He pulled both of my arms behind my back with one of his and jerked me off of the door, so he could see my tits from over my shoulder.

"Fuck, Isabella, your tits."

He rocked his hips against mine. "Feel my cock?" he asked.

I furrowed my brows, the feel of his hardness making me clench. I just wanted to feel it inside of me again, anywhere inside of me.

"Beg for me, and I'll let you suck it." He inhaled my scent and chuckled against me. "And after you suck me off, I'll fuck this tight"—he pushed his finger harder against my entrance—"little"—harder—"pussy."

"Please, Roman," I pleaded, just wanting to relax after that disaster. "I need it."

When he pushed his finger into me, I dug my claws into my office door to hold myself up and moaned loudly at the wave of pleasure that crashed over me. I wanted to feel full, feel him ram himself down my throat, making me red in the face and teary-eyed.

"Louder," he ordered. "I want everyone to know that you're moaning for me, your mate."

"Please, Roman," I said just a bit louder, moving my hips back and forth over his fingers.

He thrust them deeper inside of me and watched my tits bounce. I reached behind me, stroking my hand up and down his cock through his navy-blue suit pants.

"On your knees, my dear Isabella," he said. Once he pulled his fingers out of me, I grabbed the door handle, but Roman pulled my hand away. "I said, on your knees," he said. "Not in your office."

I turned around, eyes wide. "Out here?"

"Yes, Isabella. Out here, on your knees, staring up at me with those sexy fucking eyes."

My heart raced. I knelt in front of him and sprawled my fingers over his huge bulge. I couldn't believe that I was doing this right here, when anyone could walk around the corner, anyone could see me sucking my mate's cock.

After pulling down his zipper, he pulled out his thick, hard cock and slapped it against my lips. I wrapped my hand around the base and licked from his balls to his head as I stared up at him. I swirled my tongue around his head, gently sucking on it. He was so big, and my pussy was throbbing for it.

"Fuck my mouth?" I asked Roman, batting my lashes. "Please, Alpha."

He grabbed the sides of my head and pulled me toward him. "Touch yourself for me," he said.

When I pushed a hand between my legs and started rubbing my clit, he shoved himself all the way into my throat until his hips were pressing against my lips.

Stilling for one, two, three moments at the most, he forcefully bobbed my head back and forth on his cock until spit dripped down my chin and I couldn't stop gagging. Even then, he continued. My core clenched as I rubbed myself off.

Someone walked into the hallway behind Roman, and my nipples hardening at the thought of getting caught. I swallowed his cock, still letting him fuck my mouth, and glanced down the hall.

Kylo fucking Marks.

When he saw us, he stopped immediately and sucked in a deep breath, eyes fixed on me and my bouncing tits. I tensed and looked between the two men, my pussy tightening. It was so fucking wrong that this turned me on even more.

Instead of walking back down the hall, Kylo leaned back against the wall and crossed his arms over his chest, the corner of his lips curling into a devilish smirk. Eyes flickering gold, he bit down on his lower lip.

Roman had to know that someone was behind him, yet he continued in an animalistic manner, staring down at me and watching the tears fill my eyes as I gagged. I should've told Roman who it really was.

But I couldn't get a single word out.

With one hand, Roman reached down and pinched my nipple between my fingers. A wave of pleasure rolled through me, and I clenched again.

Moon Goddess. Moon Goddess. Moon Goddess.

Kylo placed a hand on the huge bulge in his gray suit pants, slowly moving his large hand down a good eight inches and back up. Down and back up. Down so low and back up. My pussy tightened, and I moaned on Roman's cock.

This was wrong.

"Is that all you have?" I asked when he pulled out of my throat for the first time. Drool dripped from my lips onto my sheer shirt, making it cling to my breasts.

Roman growled and thrust himself all the way down my throat, holding himself there. I gazed up at him, cheeks flushing. I placed one hand on his thigh, trying to pull away so I could breathe, yet he wrapped a hand into my hair and held me close to him.

"Is that all your fucking throat can take?" he asked back.

I wrapped my arms around the backs of his thighs and pulled myself closer to him, eyes filling to the brim with tears. I gagged on his cock, knowing that I needed to pull away soon, but he still held me in place.

"Come on, Isabella. Deeper."

Rubbing my pussy so fucking hard, I pushed him as deep as I could and choked on him. Kylo stood there, staring at us, hand in his pants, stroking his cock faster than before. He rested his head back against the wall, tensed, and let his eyes roll back, as if signaling that *he* had just come.

My pussy tightened, and I moaned on Roman's cock as a toe-curling orgasm ripped through me. Roman slowed his thrusts, grunted, and then stilled inside of me, his warm cum rolling down the back of my throat. When he pulled out of me, Kylo readjusted himself, smirked at me, and disappeared back down the hallway.

I stared down the now-empty hallway, trying to catch my breath as my wolf purred. It was wrong—so fucking wrong—

but Roman had loved every moment of it. He had never used my throat so brutally and ruthlessly before. And part of me—that feral and animalistic side of me—had loved it too.

CHAPTER 7

ROMAN

*A*fter slinging my arm around Isabella's waist, I pulled her closer to me. Sunlight flooded in through the curtains, which were billowing open with the morning breeze. Agonizing howls rattled through the open window and filled our bedroom. I tensed and sat up in bed.

Those howls weren't from wolves taking their daily runs. They were from being attacked.

War.

War was here already.

Voices from my warriors buzzed through the mind link, getting jumbled together. I shot out of bed, letting Isabella turn over.

When she heard the growls, she jumped up. "They're here already?"

"Stay here," I said to her, not wanting her to put herself in harm's way.

Kylo knew that if he took her from me, I'd be weak. And while I trusted Isabella, I didn't trust that prick anymore. His family had destroyed mine, and I wanted to destroy him for it.

When my feet hit the forest ground, I shifted into my wolf and sprinted toward the battle, following the stench of blood. From the mere sound of paws and growling, there had to be at least a hundred enemy wolves.

Shit. Shit. Shit.

Isabella followed after me despite me telling her not to. When we entered the battle, the stench of blood was even stronger. Wolves were ripping each other apart, digging their claws into flesh, latching on to shoulders and legs and paws with their teeth.

Overcome with rage, I sprinted through the pack, trying to find Kylo. If he wanted to fight, he'd fight me one-on-one, not ruthlessly kill my packmates because he had something against me.

"Roman," Isabella said, right on my ass. "Be careful. He's a Wolf Moon warrior."

"Stay here."

I couldn't keep Mom alive, but Isabella ... I would give my life for her. All I wanted was to keep her safe. *Nobody* would ever lay their hands on her.

Thank the Moon Goddess that Isabella actually obeyed me for once and stopped mid-forest, eyes glazing over; she must've been talking through her mind link to Raj. I hurried forward, searching for that piece of shit when Isabella screamed.

I turned on my heel to see a huge gash in her shoulder. She shifted into her wolf and turned to kill the man when she stopped suddenly and stared at the towering alpha behind her attacker—Kylo.

Kylo stared at her with so much ferocity, eyes with golden streaks, teeth with blood. He growled at his warrior who had hurt Isabella, watching him bow his head in submission and scurry away.

Blind with rage, I leaped in Kylo's direction and sank my teeth into the side of his neck, dragging him to the ground before he had a chance to kill Isabella himself. Nobody would take my mate away from me, especially not a cruel alpha like him.

Teeth bared at each other's necks. Sharp claws swiping through the air. Two alphas who wanted to prove their dominance.

And I'd defeat him this time. I wasn't the same naive young boy he had once known.

Blood poured from our open wounds. Kylo spit a chunk of my fur from his mouth, ran at me again, and latched his teeth into my other shoulder. I lunged my body to the side, wanting to thrust him off me yet something cracked.

I howled and collapsed, my shoulder giving out. Kylo sank his teeth further into my flesh. I kicked back with my hind leg, colliding with his groin. He growled and went to rip more flesh out of me when someone knocked him off me.

Isabella viciously threw him across the forest in the direction he had come from. Kylo immediately stood back up and growled, yet Isabella held her ground. I dug my claws into the ground, stumbling to my feet as I tried to get my shoulder bones to heal as quickly as they could.

After giving her one last long look, he lifted his nose to the trees and howled. In an instant, he and his wolves stopped engaging in combat and ran back through the woods, retreating for some ungodly reason.

He could've slaughtered every one of us.

Yet he hadn't.

I shifted into my human and clutched my shoulder, embarrassed, furious, and upset. Everything for the past few years had been building up to this moment, and I had screwed it up because Kylo had gotten in my fucking head yesterday—when I found out that he had been alone with her, when he'd told Isabella that Scarlett was trying to snatch me away from her, when I let him watch me fuck her pretty little face to show him that she was *not* to be touched in any way.

While he'd had multiple chances to end her life, he hadn't, which made me think that he was planning something much, much worse for her than an easy death. And there was one thing that was worse than a death in battle for a wolf born under the Wolf Moon.

The Wolf's Flower.

"Come on," Isabella said, nodding toward the direction of the hospital.

When we arrived, nearly every room in the hospital was filled by warriors getting their injuries treated. He hadn't even been here for twenty minutes, and he'd managed to hurt so many of our warriors.

After Isabella's mother stitched up my shoulder, I stormed out of the hospital with Isabella on my heels again.

"Listen to me, Roman," she said. "Don't be angry with me for interfering. Be thankful for me. He almost killed you. You don't have to be bold and dominant all the damn time. You can ask for help from your own mate."

I growled and shook my head. That wasn't what this was about. "You could've gotten hurt."

"Well, you would've died."

"I need to go talk to Cayden." I walked past her and toward my office.

Maybe it was a bit too much. I didn't want Isabella to be

in danger. Giving up my leadership, my natural instinct to protect my mate, was fucking hard. Dad hadn't protected Mom, and they'd both ended up buried six feet under.

We needed a strategy that wouldn't put Isabella at risk.

And I knew just the thing.

CHAPTER 8

ISABELLA

*F*or the rest of the day, Roman locked himself in his office with Cayden and our strongest warriors to strategize. I paced around in our bedroom and tried thinking of a plan of my own. How could we defeat someone so strong, so powerful …

So undeniably sexy.

I rolled my eyes and blocked out my wolf. My wolf never had anything to say, but after she had seen him fighting, how—

No, nope. I wasn't even going to go there.

I hopped off of the bed and walked out of the pack house. The moon glimmered above, seeping through the trees and creating patterns on the forest floor. I needed to run to clear my mind—that was what I told myself.

Shifting into my wolf, I sprinted toward the direction that Kylo had come from this morning. *What was wrong with him, thinking that he could just attack Roman? What were they really fighting about?*

There was no way that fight had been just over land. There had to be more. At least, Roman had surely acted like it.

Wind rushed through my fur. A gush of fresh *pine-infused* air filled my lungs. I pushed myself harder, leaping over upended tree roots and ducking under branches. My wolf guided me with ease through the forest.

I stopped when we approached a gorge, nearly slipping off the side of the cliff and falling a hundred feet into a shallow river. Rocks tumbled down the side of the mountain, smacking against the water with a loud, echoing crack.

I shifted into my human and leaned over, breathing deeply. When I stood straight, I stared over the edge and shook my head. I had mulled over ways to defeat him for hours and still couldn't come up with a single good strategy.

"Mmm, princess," someone said into my ear, brushing his fingers against my arms.

My body stiffened at the sound of Kylo's voice, and I covered my breasts with my forearm. As my wolf purred inside of me, I swallowed hard and stared into the deep, dark gorge.

"I knew you'd come find me." He drew his nose up the side of my neck, lips following so damn softly that I could barely feel them. After inhaling deeply, he pushed some hair behind my shoulder. "Moon Goddess, you smell so good. I've been waiting for you all night."

After gaining control over my wolf, I yanked myself away from him. "You need to stop."

Fully clothed with a fresh scar running through his eyebrow, he stood there with his head tilted slightly to the side. The moonlight glimmered against his chiseled jaw. "What exactly do I need to stop?"

"Whatever it is that you're up to," I said and stepped closer to him.

He crossed his huge tan arms across his chest, biceps flexing through his shirt. My gaze flickered down to them for the briefest moment, and I shook my head.

Stop it, Isabella. Stop. He's not your mate. He's just someone you have an odd connection with. Nothing more.

"If you're talking about yesterday, it was not my intention to catch you on your knees with a sopping wet cunt and a mouth stuffed full with a big cock," he said, cracking a smirk. "It's a fucking sexy thing, seeing such a commanding woman like you be conquered, surrendering power to an alpha weaker than you." He moved even closer to me to murmur into my ear, "If I'm ever given another opportunity to watch you like that again, I will."

I clenched. *I fucking clenched.* Whatever kind of game he was trying to play with me, he was damn well winning.

"You won't get the chance to watch me again," I said, digging my nails into my arms.

"You love being watched that much, don't you?" He stepped even closer to me, leaving centimeters between us. "You had to pretend to hate it when you saw it was *me* behind Roman. I don't even have to *touch* you to make you feel things that he hasn't ever made you feel."

I pressed my lips together. "Shut up, Kylo." *Before I fucking kill you.*

"I bet you were thinking about me while Roman was thrusting his cock into your throat. I bet you were wondering how good I'd feel, wondering how good a real alpha could make you feel, one who would let you be who you really are—a powerful woman who can hold her own in battle and doesn't have to feel bad about protecting her mate."

Overcome with anger, I wrapped my hand around his throat and pushed him against the nearest tree. "Stop."

"There she is," Kylo said, eyes flickering gold. "That strong warrior who craves respect from a man."

"Stop," I said louder, thoughts clouding my mind. "Stop it. Now."

"Why?" he asked, body pressed against the tree. "Are you afraid?"

I dug my claws harder into him. I could kill him right here, right now. Could end this torture. Could put myself out of the misery to come. But I didn't.

Instead, I said, "No. It's disrespectful, Kylo. I have a fucking mate that I went through hell to get with. I have built a life with him that I want to continue. I don't need a rude asshole like you screwing that up."

"Disrespectful?" He choked out a loud, lifeless laugh and pushed me away from him. "Is not believing in your abilities respectful?" He stepped closer to me, and I moved away. "Is telling you—a Lycan—to stay in the pack house while a battle is going on outside respectful?" He grasped my jaw in his hand, snapping it shut. "Huh? Do you feel respected?"

My heart raced. "Fuck you."

"They're simple questions, princess. Answer them."

I pushed him away, wanting nothing more than to have him out of my life forever. All he was doing was trying to get inside of my head, trying to make me give up everything that I had with Roman.

When I didn't say anything—because I refused to lie straight through my teeth—he clenched his jaw. "He's the kind of guy who craves dominance; he wants to be the man of the pack and looks for a woman who will make him feel like he is everything. Once you really start to lead on your own and don't need him for protection, he will force you to make yourself smaller again—*for him*. It's already taken a toll on your relationship, hasn't it?"

Staring at him with wavering eyes, I pressed my lips together. Roman had been stressed ever since the night when we killed all the rogues in their hideout. And it was aggravating to have him not believe in me after I'd proven myself over and over.

Kylo released my jaw and stepped back. "If you want me to stay away from you, I will."

I parted my lips, wanting to say something smart, and then quickly pressed them back together. Something inside of me stirred, and my wolf was quiet again, like she didn't know what to feel either.

"You don't have a problem with that, do you, princess?"

"No," I said, clenching my jaw. "Of course not."

"Good," he said, walking toward the gorge. "But just to make things clear, you're not getting rid of me that easily. I'm still coming for Roman's pack. A darkness has overcome the western part of the forest already. War has broken out. Why not add to it, princess? Force what I've been vying for, for years—Roman's downfall."

Before I had a chance to respond, Kylo took off his shirt, shifted into his wolf, and leaped with ease over the twenty-foot-wide gorge. I stared at his figure until he disappeared into the forest, and I turned on my heel.

Tugging on his shirt so I didn't have to stand naked in the forest, I padded back to the pack house in a daze. I tried hard to not let Kylo's words get to me, but he had known exactly what would stick, what would get me angry, what would make me think about *him*.

And it made me so fucking angry because Roman respected me *and* my abilities …

At times.

When I made it to the house, I ditched the shirt in the

garbage can outside. Roman was still in his office with the other high-ranking warriors from our pack. I changed into a pair of fresh clothes.

I walked into his office and slumped onto the couch. Roman lifted his nose, sniffed the air twice, and locked hard eyes on to mine. After a few moments, he pulled away and looked back toward Cayden.

"That won't work," Cayden said. "He's smart."

Derek dragged a dark hand across his tired face. "What do you suggest then?"

"Sources say that Kylo will be gone for a couple nights next week," Cayden said. "It will be our chance to attack his territory when he's weak and unguarded. Kill his warriors, so he has nobody to protect him when he comes home, and then we can finally kill him after all these years."

Kill him?

Vanessa crossed her arms over her chest, pushing her breasts together. "Isn't that kind of dishonorable?"

"If he's dead, he's dead. Isn't that right, my dear Isabella?" Roman gazed at me as if he knew everything that had happened when I went out for a run or yesterday, when Kylo and I chatted or when Kylo watched me suck him off.

My eyes widened slightly, yet I found myself nodding along despite my wolf whimpering. She needed to shut the hell up; I couldn't stand her desperateness for him anymore. When we were close to him, she was quiet and ashamed. When Roman talked about killing him, she was sad and angry. She needed to make up her damn mind because I had made up mine.

My mind was Roman. It would always be Roman.

Roman walked around the desk to stand next to me, his fingers brushing against mine. "And after we destroy his pack, you can do the honors of killing him, Isabella." He looked to everyone for the briefest moment. "You're dismissed."

When everyone left the room, Roman grazed his fingers against my jaw, his touch so unusually gentle. "I want to apologize for getting angry with you earlier. I just … it made me feel helpless when you stood in front of me and bared your teeth at him." He brushed his fingers against my hips and pulled me closer. "I know that you're strong, Isabella. I just want to protect you with my life. I don't want you to have the same fate my mom did."

I frowned at him, my heart aching with guilt. How could I have let Kylo instill all those little thoughts into me again? What was my wolf's problem with him? Why did she trust him so innately, like one would a mate?

Roman stared at me with those same big golden eyes that I had fallen in love with every time I opened my curtains and stared out into the forest.

I swept my fingers across his forehead, pushing dark locks of hair off his face. "I won't end up like your mother. I know how much that hurt you."

"Let me protect you then," he pleaded with his lips on mine. "Please."

"Not if you're putting your own life in danger, Roman. I will not let you die for me when I can stop someone from killing you," I said.

He inhaled softly through his mouth and hesitated. He didn't say anything. He didn't nod but didn't shake his head either.

I grasped his hands in mine and brought them to my lips. "I love you. More than anything. We're in this war together."

Lips twitching into a hesitant smile, he pushed his fingers against the front of my pants. "Let me show you how much I love you," he said, slipping them inside and toying with my folds.

I arched a brow, laughter bubbling out of me. "I thought you loved me more than *this*."

After growling lowly in my ear, he snaked a hand around my throat and pinned me against the door. When his stubble brushed against my mark, I shivered in delight and clenched.

"I don't need to moan Cayden's name again to get you to fuck me, do I?"

"Try it, Isabella. See where your bratty mouth gets you."

"Cay—"

Someone knocked on the door.

"Isabella?" Raj said.

"Moon Goddess." I swore under my breath and frowned. "Not now."

"Isabella is busy, Raj," Roman said. "She'll talk to you tomorrow."

My lips curled into a smile, my heart racing inside my chest. Roman stared down at me, full lips parting. I furrowed my brows, a wave of pleasure warming my core.

Faster, I mouthed to him.

Raj sighed deeply and knocked again. "This is important. It can't wait."

Roman moved his fingers faster, nearly bringing me to my orgasm, and then stopped. He smirked down at me, pulled out his fingers, and sucked them right into his mouth. "I'll be waiting in our room for you. Don't be long."

I stood breathlessly in the middle of the doorway as Roman walked out. Raj walked in and shut the door behind himself, too calm and collected that it scared me. I straightened myself out and sat at Roman's desk.

Raj tossed a file onto Roman's desk, filled with pictures of Kylo and me that seemed to have been taken *tonight*. "Do you have anything that you need to tell me?" Raj asked.

"No," I said slowly, unsure of where he was going with this.

"Well"—he sat across from me with a tight jaw—"I have questions for *you*." He grabbed papers from the file, not even bothering to look at them, and scooped them up. "What were you doing, out with Kylo in the middle of the night, alone?"

"How did you find out about that?" I asked. It had happened less than an hour ago.

"Since Ryker, I've raised the security on everyone in the Lycans, including you." He stood and stared down at me with sorrowful eyes. "Just tell me, Isabella. You were hated the man a few hours ago. Why were you meeting with him without informing me?"

I wrapped my arms around my body. "I went out on a run. My wolf guided me toward his property. She has … this connection with him that I don't quite understand." I gazed down at the oak desk, overcome with guilt, and frowned. "I really want to understand why my wolf is drawn to him even though I despise everything that he is."

Raj stared at me for a few moments, swallowed, and nodded. "Okay," he said quietly, sitting back down. I could tell that he didn't want to be fucked over by a leader again, and I didn't blame him. "Good."

"I'm glad that you have security watching me," I said because I didn't trust my wolf with him, especially when she had been begging me to let him touch us the entire walk home. "My wolf is scaring me. Do you think this is related to us both being born under the Wolf Moon?"

Raj blew out a breath and stared out the window at the deep night sky. "Possibly. There is a celebration for the Wolf Moon every year. I'm not sure if you know about it. We've been so swamped with work lately that I think I forgot to give you the invitation. But it's where all of the adult wolves born during that time come together to celebrate the Moon Goddess and the strength she granted the Wolf Moon warriors."

"I heard stories about it when I was younger," I said, gnawing on the inside of my lip.

"If you're worried about your wolf's connection with Kylo, you should go to that celebration and see if you can get answers. Only Wolf Moon wolves are invited to attend, and it's rumored that the Moon Goddess herself—or one of her divine wolves—makes an appearance."

My eyes widened. "So, you're suggesting I go?" I shook my head. "There's no way. I can't."

Nearly an hour ago, I'd almost turned back around, jumped across the gorge, and run to Kylo's pack. I had almost lost control, almost let his words sway me. There was no way I could trust my wolf to be somewhere alone with him again.

"Roman plans to attack Kylo's pack during that time," I said. "I need to stay."

"You are aware that *it is against the law* to engage in any attack on a pack during the Wolf Moon celebration weekend."

I gnawed on the inside of my lip again, tearing at the skin. It might've been against the law, but Raj didn't know who Roman really was. Roman would do anything to defend his pack, would do anything to protect me, especially after his parents died.

In Roman's mind, attacking Kylo's pack while he was gone to celebrate the Wolf Moon seemed to be the only way to get the advantage because Kylo was clearly stronger than Roman.

"You're not going to miss a chance to meet the divine wolves or the Moon Goddess just because of Kylo and Roman's war," Raj said. "You're going. I'll take care of the Lycans while you're gone."

I guessed it was settled. I was going to attend.

My wolf purred. *We're going to see Kylo.*

CHAPTER 9

ROMAN

*W*hen Isabella had walked into my office earlier, she'd had a profuse pine fragrance all over her body, drifting around the room like a fucking ghost taunting me. At the time, my wolf had been so overcome with anger and fear that I couldn't think straight.

Pulling out thick black rope that I kept in our closet to tie Isabella up, I tossed it on the bed and cut my eyes to the door as she walked into the room with her lips curled into a small smile.

Now that I'd had time to sit in our room without her, I knew whose scent it was.

"Take off your clothes and get onto the bed, Isabella."

She walked toward the bed and hopped up onto it, kicking her legs back and forth. "No."

"No?" I asked, voice strained. I stepped toward her, trying hard to calm my wolf because all he wanted to do was devour every inch of her, prove to her that he was enough, leave her so satisfied that she couldn't physically stand for weeks.

With that bratty mouth, she smirked. "No."

I wrapped my hand around her throat, pulled her to her feet, turned her around, and pushed her against our bedroom door, my chest against her back. Taking a deep breath, I inhaled that fucking asshole's scent and growled, "Yes."

After tearing her shirt at the seams, I looped my fingers around the band of her bra and did the same thing, watching her breasts bounce under the dim moonlight shining through the window.

"No." She struggled against me, but I could just feel her perky ass tighten.

"You do as I say, my dear Isabella." I strummed my fingers against her fragile neck. "No defying me." I yanked down her pants and released her just enough so she could move. "Now, grab the fucking rope and hand it over to me."

"No."

She was testing my damn patience tonight. More than I fucking wanted her to.

"Do you want me to be hard on you?" I asked through my canines.

"Hard on me?" She rolled her eyes, fucking knowing that it'd piss me off. "You never go hard on me."

Once I threw her onto the bed, I snatched the rope and her left thigh. I tied the thick cord around her ankle, then that same rope to her wrist, and then to the bed post, so every part of her cunt was spread open for me to take how *I* wanted.

Struggling some more, she pushed me away when I grabbed her other ankle. I slapped my bare palm against her pussy and watched her body jerk up in surprise. I seized her ankle and wrist, tying them to the other post.

Callous fingers gliding up her smooth thighs, I pulled her

ass off the bed and let my spit drip from my lips onto her clit. The spit rolled down her mound to her entrance and then ever lower to her tight asshole.

I rubbed the wetness around her clit. "Look at this pussy glisten."

She squirmed in my hands, legs slowly starting to tremble.

"This pussy is mine." I stared up at her, letting my wolf take control of me. I trailed my nose up her inner thigh, inhaling the scent of her untainted cunt. At least this didn't smell like Kylo too. I growled against her folds, "Tell me it's mine, Isabella."

She shook her head, defying me yet again. "No."

I slapped her across the pussy again. "Tell me it's fucking mine."

"No."

Another smack, this time harder. "I'm not going to ask you again."

"No."

Again, I slapped her pussy, making it bright red.

Entire body jerking into the air, she furrowed her brows in a lustful stare. I smacked her again.

"Mine," I growled, sitting up and positioning my cock right at her entrance. "Tell me you're fucking mine."

"I'm yours, Roman! All fucking yours," she screamed out.

Unable to hold back, I shoved my cock into her sopping pussy until she was gripping me so desperately. Grabbing the backs of her thighs, I held them even further apart as I thrust in and out of her.

After placing an openmouthed kiss on her lips, I marked her body by leaving blotchy red hickeys down her chest and breasts. She arched her back, and I rammed myself harder into her until she was tugging on the restraints.

"Please, Roman! I'm going to come. Please, let me come."

"Don't fucking come," I said, driving my cock into her pussy.

Every time I pulled it out, she tightened just a bit more, squeezing my cock like she wanted me to pump my entire load of cum into her.

Suddenly, her pussy quivered, and she got quiet.

I pulled myself all the way out of her and slapped her across the pink pussy again. "I said"—smack—"not to"—smack—"come." I wrapped my hand around her throat and pulled her up a few inches.

She grabbed the ropes in her hands and tugged on them. "Please, Roman. Please, I need it. Put your cum inside of me and fill me up. I'm so desperate for it."

I grunted and buried myself deep into her. "Fucking come for me, Isabella."

She cried out, her pussy pulsing around my cock and swallowing my cum. I brushed my fingers across her collarbone and frowned down at my mate, hurting at the thought of her not telling me about meeting the man I hated the most.

Since the moment I'd turned eighteen and laid my eyes on her, I had fallen in love.

When Mom and Dad had been murdered in the middle of my freshman year, I had to be the ruthless alpha that my father had been, had to be cruel and heartless, had to kill without mercy and protect without thought. But when Isabella had shown up to one of my practices to watch the warriors fight, I'd vowed to protect her from everything.

Now … now, she was willingly putting herself in harm's way and hiding it from me.

She glanced out the window and toward the woods. So, I had to get rid of him sooner rather than later. I couldn't wait for Kylo to snatch up my mate one day.

Avoiding eye contact, I undid her restraints, pulled on

some clothes, and grabbed my phone. "Next time you meet with Kylo behind my back, remember the way you beg for my cock, Isabella."

I stormed out of the room before I lost complete control of my wolf and dialed Cayden's number. "Tell me you have information on the Wolf's Flower."

CHAPTER 10

ISABELLA

*A*ll the ecstasy running through my body evaporated when Roman stormed out of the room and slammed the door behind him. I stared wide-eyed at the moonflowers sparkling on our windowsill until tears filled my eyes. The hurt in Roman's voice and the guilt I felt about my wolf's connection to Kylo slowly ravaged my heart.

How could I explain something like this to Roman? I could tell him the truth—that I had gone out on a run and Kylo found me. But he'd want to know why I hadn't told him as soon as I saw him.

Moon Goddess, I'd wanted to tell him the truth more than anything, but I didn't know how to explain my connection with the man he hated the most. If Roman found out about it, he'd run into another battle, blind with rage.

My heart ached, my wolf whimpering. I tugged on some clothes and pushed the sudden tears from my eyes, hesitantly opening the hallway door to see Roman pacing back and forth down the hall with his phone pressed to his ear.

"It could kill Isabella?" he asked, not seeing me yet.

With my arms crossed over my chest, I stepped closer to him and cleared my throat. "Roman, can we talk?" I asked even though it killed me on the inside.

I hated confrontation. We had been through so much already, and I just wanted a peaceful life.

Roman held up a single finger. "Wait."

I walked closer to him, trying to listen in on his phone call.

"You think he has the fucking flower? How do you know for sure?" Roman asked, brows furrowed, putting the phone on speaker. "Who told you?"

"Scarlett," Cayden said.

"Why are you talking to Scarlett?" I asked, balling my hands into fists.

She wasn't in our pack, and I didn't like her trying to get close again to Roman. She had been all fucking over him at the Lycans' alpha meeting the other day.

"She was hanging in The Night Raider's Café earlier this evening. Some of our warriors overheard her talking about the flower," Cayden said. He paused for two beats. "I think that Kylo has taken the Wolf's Flower from Scarlett. She apparently kept saying that he stole it from her. I don't know if she's telling the truth or trying to stir up trouble. Chaos has seemed to have overtaken her pack. The alpha was killed shortly after the meeting yesterday, and people are fighting for power."

"What's the Wolf's Flower?" I asked.

Roman sighed with annoyance through his nose and pressed his lips together, only making me angrier.

I growled, "Don't keep important things from me, Roman. I need to know."

Roman growled back at me, "You kept your little meeting with Kylo from me."

I suppressed the urge to roll my eyes. It sounded like we were in the fifth grade with all this jealousy between us, but I knew that this was my fault. Roman was reacting this way because of me.

"It's a scientifically modified flower," Cayden interrupted. "It was made to weaken those born under the Wolf's Moon if they drink or eat part of it. Basically, it's a poison that could kill a Wolf Moon wolf within moments."

Roman clenched his fists, his jaw twitching. "Scarlett took the Wolf's Flower from my family when my parents died. I have been trying to get it back ever since. My mother had kept it in her possession because she knew that if it fell into the wrong hands, it would be turned into a weapon against the strongest wolves on earth."

"Who modified the flower, and why?"

"It was produced over hundreds of years ago by someone named Dolus," Cayden said through the phone. "Legend says he was a werewolf hunter, but I don't know if that's true. He created it to wipe out all wolves like you."

"Now, Kylo fucking has it."

"You think he's going to use it on me?" I asked, my wolf slowly starting to anger.

"Of course he would!" Roman snapped at me, eyes flickering gold. "He's deceptive, and you're blindly falling into the little traps he's set for you to get you to trust him, like you sneaking out at night to see him."

Cayden cleared his throat. "I'll call you back later." The line went dead.

Roman stuffed his phone back into his pocket, staring at me with eyes filled with rage and heartbreak—the same expression I had seen when I told him that I would leave him for a year to become a Lycan.

"All I wanted was to go for a run. He must've followed me out there. I didn't intentionally meet him. I told him to stay away from us and from me, that we're mates and that nothing will come between us."

"I'm trying to fucking protect you, Isabella."

"Well, let me protect you for once, Roman. I stopped Kylo from killing you, and you are still upset about it. All I told him was to not get in the way of our relationship again."

"He could've killed you if he had that damn flower when you talked to him," he said. Roman blew an angry breath out of his nose, pushed a hand through his hair, and asked, "What is Kylo to you?"

I stared at Roman, surprised at the mere question, and shook my head. "Nothing."

"What is he?" he repeated, this time tense.

"Nothing," I said, but my wolf was quiet. So desperately quiet.

"Then, you won't mind if I take the Wolf's Flower from him and kill him with it, right?" Roman asked.

My canines ripped through my gums, and my wolf let out a ferocious and possessive growl. It happened so quickly and so explosively that it scared *me*. I forced myself to sprint right out of the house before she could hurt Roman because I felt like she was about to foam at the teeth from the mere mention of killing Kylo.

CHAPTER 11

ISABELLA

*C*alm *down,* I demanded my wolf.

She pushed me to run faster and faster until I found myself standing outside Vanessa's secluded cabin on the outskirts of Roman's property. I needed someone to talk to about this, preferably female because I wasn't sure if Derek would understand.

After knocking, I waited a few moments. She appeared in a skimpy set of red lingerie with a bottle of wine in her hand and a huge grin on her face. "Lindsey, you're—" she started. When she caught sight of *me*, she stopped and widened her eyes. "Oh, Isabella." She gazed down at my naked body, her cheeks flushing pink. "Come in."

"I'm not bothering you, am I?"

She handed me a silky black robe from her faux velvet couch, and I pulled it on to cover my body. "Don't worry about it. I didn't have any plans for tonight." She set her wine down on the table, sent a quick text, and grabbed another robe from her room to cover herself. "What's wrong?"

"I need someone to talk to," I said.

My whole world felt like it was falling apart. Not only was my wolf hung up on Kylo for some ungodly reason, but also all I could feel was Roman's pain when I sprinted away from him. I loved him with my entire heart, and I didn't want to lose him over this senseless feeling inside of me.

"Come on," she said, nodding to the other room.

I followed her to the kitchen, gazing around her small, cozy home. For someone who had made my life in high school absolute hell, I hadn't expected her house to be so … homey.

A vanilla candle burned on the counter as she popped the cork on the wine. She had cute little moonflowers on her windowsill, just like I did at home. And there were a variety of pictures on her refrigerator.

I ambled over to it, gazing at each one as she poured us wine. There was a picture of her and Jane hugging each other in their pink pajamas and one of her training with the warriors, and near the top of the fridge was a picture of her and me on the night that I'd become leader of the Lycans.

"This is so cute." I smiled at the picture, feeling warm on the inside.

After handing me a glass of wine, she tied the robe tighter around her tiny waist and shifted back and forth on her feet. "That was the best night of my life."

"That night was the best night of your life?" I asked. "We had been chased by hordes of rogues."

She grinned at me, looped her arm around mine, and rested her head on my shoulder. "But I had the chance to work with you for the first time." She brushed her thumb against the image. "It was the first night that I felt like you appreciated me and looked at me differently." She frowned and turned toward me. "Isabella, I never told you this, but I'm sorry for making your life hell in high school."

"It's okay," I said.

Our relationship was much better now despite everything.

She shook her blonde hair. "No, it's not. I made your life literal hell."

I let out a laugh, which felt good after what had happened back at the pack house. "Yeah, you did, but the past is the past. We're good now."

Light from the candle flickered against her tan face as she smiled and tugged me to the living room, where we collapsed onto the couch. She nudged me. "Tell me what happened. What's wrong?"

My lips parted and quivered. I placed the wine down on the coffee table and curled my knees to my chest. "Roman," I croaked out. My heart ached so damn bad at the thought of hurting him *and* at the thought of him killing Kylo.

A tree branch hit the window, and I pressed a hand to my chest.

Vanessa frowned at me and pushed some hair from my face, enveloping me into a hug. "It's just the wind. Go on."

My body trembled as I curled up next to her. "I love him. I love him so fucking much that it hurts to hurt him," I whispered. "But my wolf is drawn to another wolf. She can't help herself when it comes to him. She feels so connected for some reason."

Vanessa tensed for a moment and then stroked my hair. She parted her lips to say something but then snapped them shut. I didn't expect her to say anything because if I were her, I wouldn't know what to say either.

Instead, she let me cry some more in her arms and nudged me when I calmed down. "Let's take your mind off of Roman for a couple hours. We can watch my favorite show."

I pushed away my last tear and arched a brow. "And what's that?"

"*Murder Mystery.*"

I curled my arm around hers. "Of course it is."

Sunlight blazed through the sheer orange curtains. I woke up on the couch with an aching back and a sore neck. Vanessa was lying on top of me, her eyes closed peacefully and her head on my stomach.

My lips curled into a small smile. I didn't feel better, but I was glad that I had a friend. These past few weeks had been so lonely. So many people depended on me, and so many people only talked to me because they needed something from me. I hadn't hung out with Derek at all because our schedules didn't line up. So … I blew out a deep breath … I'd needed this.

Careful not to wake Vanessa, I slid off the couch and ran to The Night Raider's Café to pick up her favorite chocolate strudel. After placing it on her coffee table and leaving a thank-you note, I ran to the Lycans' property to find Raj.

So much had happened last night that I needed to tell him about.

Sitting in my office with one ankle propped up on his knee, he tapped his fingers to a beat on my desk. "Morning, killer."

"I have information."

He arched a brow at me. "You look like shit. No offense."

"None taken." I collapsed into my chair. I probably should've gone back to the pack house, so Roman knew I was okay, but I couldn't get myself to see him this morning. "Roman and I had a fight over Kylo last night. He told me that Kylo has a flower called the Wolf's Flower, which could kill a wolf born under the Wolf's Moon. He thinks that Kylo will try to use it on me."

Raj blew out a deep breath. "Why didn't we know about this?"

"Ryker probably knew about it," I said, shaking my head at the thought of him keeping so much from us. "Either way, we can't let Roman get it or let Kylo keep it. It is safest with the Lycans."

"You don't trust Roman with it?"

No, he'll kill our Kylo.

I tensed and swallowed hard, cheeks flushing. *Our Kylo?*

After pushing my wolf out of my mind, I sat up taller. "He can't have it."

Raj sat back and furrowed his brows, intertwining his brown fingers. "If he has that flower and it really does what Roman says it does, I don't think you should attend the party. I know I said that you should go, but I don't want you to be in danger. And I'm sure that Roman won't let you go after finding that out."

Yet something inside told me that Kylo wasn't a threat *to me.*

"Kylo won't hurt me."

He hadn't hurt me at the meeting. He hadn't hurt me during the battle. He hadn't killed me last night. Why would he wait until the party? Wouldn't he want to kill me in front of Roman, where he could gloat in glory?

"I'm going," I said, making up my mind. "I need to find out his true intentions." And about why I was so attached to him. Maybe the Moon Goddess or one of the divine wolves would have some insight about us.

CHAPTER 12

ROMAN

*I*sabella hadn't come home last night and hadn't even come by this morning.

Find mate, my wolf demanded. *Find our mate now.*

I balled the stem of a moonflower in my hand and listened to it crack. When I had mentioned killing Kylo last night, she'd bared her canines and growled possessively at me, like the man meant something to her.

He couldn't. He fucking couldn't. She was mine.

A petal fell off the flower, drifted through the air, and landed on the oak desk, its light dimming by the moment until it went out completely.

I had run all around the pack last night, trying to find her and caught her conversation with Vanessa through the open living room window.

She had confessed that Kylo *did* mean something to her wolf.

And it'd fucking hurt to have to overhear it.

Was I not enough for her? Did Kylo feel the same way? Were they somehow ... *mates*?

All these questions had plagued my mind throughout the night, kept me awake when I should've been asleep and preparing for another battle or trying desperately to get that flower to protect my Isabella.

I had fought to be the man Isabella needed *and* wanted for years. I wasn't going to let Kylo take her away from me like this. I couldn't. If I lost her, I wouldn't know what to do with myself, didn't know what kind of man I would become.

What was an alpha without his mate? Nothing.

He was nothing.

The front door opened, and I shot up from my seat. "Isabella!" I called from my office, keeping my wolf under control so I didn't push her away by sounding too angry or by being too overprotective, like she hated.

She pitter-pattered through the house.

Get mate, my wolf ordered. *Get her now.*

I resisted the urge to run out into the hallway, grab her by the wrist, and tell her never to go out alone on runs again because I didn't want her to be alone while that flower was in Kylo's possession. After watching rogues cut into Mom's neck, tear out her throat, and die while Dad was fighting off another somewhere in the forest, it was so difficult for *me* and my wolf to let Isabella run free.

She might not think so, but I was working on it. I really was.

"Isabella!" I shouted again, my heart racing.

Every night that she was out with the Lycans, I lay awake, just thinking the worst: *Is she hurt? Is she being chased by blood-hungry rogues too? Will I wake up to her dead on my front steps?*

Isabella walked into the hallway in front of my office with her arms crossed. "What do you want, Roman?"

After demanding that my wolf stay quiet, I stepped

toward her and lightly grasped her chin in my hand, stroking her jaw with my thumb. "You didn't come home last night."

"I know."

"I was worried."

"You're always worried."

I swallowed hard to suppress a growl. "Why didn't you answer me when I mind-linked you this morning?"

She yanked herself out of my grip. "Because I had work to do, Roman. In case you've forgotten, I'm the leader of the Lycans, not just a mate who can be at your beck and call whenever you want to get frisky." She paused for a moment and then slumped her shoulders forward, defeated. "I'm sorry. I shouldn't have said that. I'm tired, sore, and upset."

Reaching out for her hand, I brushed my fingers against hers. "I don't expect you to be here all day. I know you have work to do with the Lycans, but I can't go hours without hearing from you. I need to know that you're safe."

When she closed her eyes, she pulled her fingers away from me. "Trust me."

"If you want me to trust you, tell me who he is to you," I whispered, needing to get it out.

All I wanted was for her to come out and admit it to me. I didn't want to bring up that I'd overheard her conversation. I didn't want to hear her lie to me anymore. I wanted her to be honest because this was eating me up on the inside.

Chin trembling, Isabella gazed up at me with teary eyes. I waited patiently for her, even when the tears started falling and she had to wrap her arms around her body to stop herself from shaking.

"I don't want to say it out loud," she whispered.

"Tell me," I gently pleaded with her.

"You're going to get jealous over it, and I hate when you get that way."

I grasped her hands, needing to touch her, and held them tight to my chest. "I promise that I won't, my dear Isabella."

Her lips quivered, and she looked away from me. "My wolf feels connected to his. I don't know why, and I don't know how. We've mated with you, yet she ..." She paused. "She wants him too."

My heart shattered, broke into tiny little pieces, yet I held myself together for her. Moonlight glimmered into the room and shone off her hair. I tucked some behind her ear, my pulse racing.

"Do you still love me?" I whispered. "Does your *wolf* still love me?"

She wrapped her arms around my torso tightly and pulled me to her, resting her ear right above my heart. "Of course we do. You're our mate, Roman. I couldn't love anyone more than I love you."

I pulled her closer to me, rested my chin on her head, and let a tear fall down my cheek. It wasn't a sad tear, but a relieved one. My mate still wanted us. She loved us more than anyone. She wouldn't let us go.

"That's why I'm going to the Wolf Moon party this weekend," she said, clutching on to me.

I tensed at the mention of the one party that only warriors born under the Wolf Moon could attend, which meant that Kylo would be there, alone with my mate, for an entire weekend.

"I need to go to figure out why I feel this way about him," she continued.

"You can't go," I said, feeling my wolf stir under my skin. "He still has the flower. He'll try to kill you with it—slip it into your drink or force it into your mouth while you're sleeping. I can't lose you, Isabella."

She pulled away slightly. "I need to go. I leave tomorrow morning."

"Isabella, you can't. He'll kill you."

"Why are you so adamant that he'll try to kill me? We've been alone twice now, and he hasn't tried once," she said to me, grasping my face in her hands and following the streak mark from my tear with her gaze. "Help me understand, Roman."

Horrifying memories from years ago raced through my mind. I had tried to suppress them for so long because it was shameful. I was embarrassed of how I'd acted back then, when I hadn't known any better.

"I hurt Kylo in the past," I said. "He'll want to get back at me now that I have a mate."

"How'd you hurt him?"

"You don't need to know."

"Please, Roman. Don't leave me in the dark again. Let me in."

After sighing through my nose, I decided to open up all my regrets. "Scarlett was Kylo's mate, and I took her from him." I clenched my jaw and gazed at Isabella. "Before any of us turned eighteen, I used to sleep with Scarlett while Kylo watched. It was our thing. When Kylo turned eighteen and found out that Scarlett was his mate, some shit happened, and Scarlett dumped him for me."

Isabella slowly released her hold on me and defensively crossed her arms over her chest to put space between us. "You slept with Scarlett more than once?" She shook her head and mumbled how that was a stupid question under her breath. "But ... but even after you knew they were mates?"

"Isabella, I ..." I tried to find words for it, wanted to tell her that it was my biggest regret. "My parents had both just died, and I ... I felt so lonely. I was young and wasn't thinking about how hurt he would be, just how hurt I felt."

She backed away from me when I moved toward her. "You didn't respect the mate bond at all?" she asked me, hurt so strong in her voice. "Did our first time … did it mean anything to you? If you didn't care about them, why would you care about us?"

"Us being together means everything to me," I said. "I'm sorry I didn't wait to—"

"I don't care that you didn't wait to have sex with me, but a mate bond is so sacred. Knowing that they were mates and still sleeping with her … that's …" She rubbed a hand over her face and shook her head. "I don't even know how to feel."

I squeezed my eyes closed. "It's one of my deepest regrets," I admitted, feeling so ashamed.

There had been so much going on in my life at that moment, so much pain. I'd wanted to hurt Kylo for what his father had done to my parents and their relationship, their lives even.

When Isabella wrapped her arms around me, I tensed. I hadn't expected her to touch me after what I had admitted. I hadn't expected her to even want to sleep in the same bed with me tonight. I'd expected her to walk out and not come back until Monday—after the Wolf Moon party.

But she stared up at me with those big blue eyes that I had fallen in love with and said, "I still love you. The past is the past, Roman. I know you're a better man now." She kissed me on my lips, grabbed my hand, and pulled me toward the door. "Before I leave for the weekend, make love to me tonight and show me how much you care."

CHAPTER 13

KYLO

"$\mathcal{I}$ want double security around the borders when I'm gone," I said.

I gathered some papers in my office for my beta, Roger, to read about the chaos arising near Scarlett's pack. She could die for all I cared, but whatever had been going on was spreading to packs closer to mine. And nobody was going to ruin everything I had rebuilt after my father tainted our family name.

Roger grabbed the papers, glancing down at them for a moment, and nodded.

"And nobody comes within a hundred meters of the property without you knowing about it."

Roger sat on the black velvet sofa across from my desk, propping one leg onto the glass coffee table. "I don't know why you're making a huge deal out of this. It's against divine law to attack during the annual celebration of the Wolf Moon warriors. Roman respects law."

After stuffing some papers into my brown leather briefcase, I growled, "He will do anything for Isabella and anything to get back at me for what my father did to his family. He might respect divine law, but he's angry and jealous. He will attack."

I had known Roman for years. That man hadn't changed.

"Then, stay and kill him now before he has a chance to hurt you for what your parents—"

"You're not going to change my mind," I said to Roger, claws slashing into my palms in an attempt to stay calm.

I couldn't waste my chance at spending one weekend alone with Isabella. My wolf wouldn't allow it. He had been riled up this entire week, thinking about the way she'd looked in my shirt while heading home from the gorge the other night. She had lifted the thin fabric to her nose and inhaled deeply, her blue eyes overcome with a wave of golden wolfish lust when she did.

Mate, my wolf said. *We will see mate.*

Clenching my jaw, I growled at the sound of that foolish word.

We don't have a mate anymore, I scolded. *Not after Scarlett.*

Yet my wolf went on.

Mate. Mate. Isabella is—

A Wolf Moon warrior. That's it. She means nothing to us.

But that was a lie. Less than four days ago, I had met her, and I hadn't been able to stop thinking about her since. She was incredibly intelligent, was the only person I had faced who made me actually back down from a fight, and was my ex–best friend's mate.

After clearing my throat, I looked back at Roger. "I'm going to the party to see if Isabella will tell me about Roman's plans to attack. I need to know if I can trust her."

Moonlight flooded in through the windows. It was nearly one a.m. I'd have to leave at six a.m. if I wanted to get there in time for the gathering at nine a.m. A weekend full of war talk, training, and worshipping our goddess was a few hours away, and so was Isabella.

"Why do you need to trust her?"

I walked closer to the window and gazed out at the trail of moonflowers leading from the pack house into the forest toward the gorge. Isabella loved moonflowers; she had decorated the entire Lycan pack house with them.

"Because Roman doesn't deserve her," I said.

"That doesn't answer my question."

"It doesn't need to answer the question, Roger. That's my answer." I tucked my hands into my pockets. "Go home. I need to get some rest before I leave in the morning."

He hopped off the couch and threw me a lighthearted smirk. "Rest? You'll probably go running through the woods tonight, trying to find her."

My canines lengthened. "Know your boundaries."

When Roger shut the door behind him, I turned back to the window, rested my forehead against the glass, and took a deep breath. Last time my wolf had felt this connection with someone, Scarlett was my mate.

Isabella wasn't. She couldn't be.

After a few moments of convincing my wolf that we wouldn't try to find her in the woods, I opened my closet door and dialed the code on my safe. Opening it up, the Wolf's Flower sat peacefully in the center along with some extraneous papers. It had been there for nearly a month now.

Just like the Wolf Moon warriors, the flower could survive in even the worst conditions.

I carefully pulled the container top off and stared at it in amazement. This flower could destroy someone born under the Wolf Moon in seconds. It would burn them from the inside out, terrorize every part of them, hurt them more than going through heat ever could.

Once I placed it back into the container, I walked to my bedroom and stuffed it away in my suitcase. I was going to bring it to the party. For the one and only Isabella.

CHAPTER 14

ISABELLA

"*H*ow'd Roman take it when you left this morning?" Raj asked as we walked through the forest.

Hoots and howls drifted into the woods from beyond the large stone gates twenty yards ahead, where the Wolf Moon party was being held.

Supposedly, the property was a beautiful northern estate with lush green forest, large pink tulip fields, and a glimmering lake with a waterfall. While I hadn't been here before, I'd brushed up on the landscape's layout this morning in case Kylo tried something on me, like Roman had suggested.

"I don't want to talk about it," I said, approaching the guards.

When I'd left Roman this morning, he had still been sleeping. I placed a kiss on his forehead and stroked his thick brown hair that seemed to always curl onto his forehead. I had cried almost the entire way to the Lycans' to meet Raj because I loved Roman so much and didn't want whatever I had with Kylo to get in the way.

"That bad, huh?" Raj asked.

I shrugged and stood in line to gain entry onto the estate.

One of the guards nodded toward me. "Isabella, you may enter, but"—he turned to Raj—"you must leave."

Raj nodded and pulled me in for a hug. "If Kylo tries anything on you, run," Raj whispered into my ear. "Don't drink or eat anything that he gives you. If he has that flower—"

"I know," I said, rubbing his shoulder. "I won't do anything stupid."

After saying good-bye, I walked under the archway of moonflowers, beyond the gates, and into a beautiful tulip garden that seemed to stretch for miles. Someone grabbed my suitcase and handed me a glass of wine and keys to Cabin #5.

Sipping the wine, I looked around at the warriors. Some I recognized from surrounding packs while others must've lived far, far away. Years of battle, blood, and war stood around peaceful, soft pink flowers that swayed in the breeze. Every one of us had been through so much at such early ages. There were so many stories to tell, and I couldn't wait to hear Kylo's.

My fingers grazed against the tulips as I walked farther into the garden. The blazing orange sun beat down on my face, and I smiled in its warmth. Purring, my wolf led me deeper into the maze of hedges and flowers until we disappeared from the group.

Dragging me through the lush pinks and greens, gazing lovingly at the moonflowers twinkling in every which direction, sniffing the sweet scent of the tulips mixed with pine, my wolf continued.

When we turned a corner, I stopped us dead in our tracks. Kylo stood alone, staring out at the nearly endless garden and swirling his drink around in his hand, thumb brushing against some petals and muscles flexed against his thin gray button-up shirt.

My wolf purred again, and I sucked in a breath.

This entire time, she hadn't been enjoying the sight. She had been bringing me to him.

"Isabella," Kylo said without turning around. "Miss me so much that you decided to come find me?"

"I'm not here for you," I said, crossing my arms over my chest.

As he turned, my breath caught in the back of my throat. Eyes so golden, brown hair blowing softly in the wind, early morning sun bouncing off his sculpted face, he smiled so genuinely at me. "Your wolf brought you to me."

"No, she didn't." Lie. "I am here because I need answers to my questions."

When he stepped toward me, I moved back, out of fear that my wolf would react too submissively to him. She had fallen under his little trance one too many times, and I would not drop my guard again. Not after Roman's warning of him having the flower that could kill me.

"Scared of me now?" he asked, brow arched.

"I'm not scared of you." I tightened my jaw and narrowed my eyes. "I'm furious that you'd keep the Wolf's Flower from me, the one thing that could kill me within seconds. Did you plan on getting close to me, so you could kill me with it?"

"Did Roman tell you that I was going to use it on you?" After grabbing my glass from my hand and placing both of ours on a stone bench, he crossed his huge arms over his chest. "If I wanted you dead, I would've killed you myself. There have been plenty of times that I could've snatched you by the throat"—he grabbed the front of my throat with one large, callous hand—"and ripped it right out." He squeezed my neck lightly, making me feel so light-headed yet so … so … exhilarated.

"So you do have the flower."

He brushed his thumb over my jaw. "Of course I have the flower. I'm not going to let Roman kill me with it. He doesn't know how powerful it truly is, that if you even touch it the wrong way, it could blow you to pieces."

Clenching my jaw, I pushed my hands against his chest yet didn't shove him away.

Touch him more, my wolf said. *Touch all of him.*

"I brought it for you," Kylo said.

"To try to *blow me to pieces?*" I asked, compensating for all the innate desire my wolf felt for him. It wasn't that I didn't want to trust him. It was that he wasn't supposed to make me feel this way. I didn't like it, and I sure as hell wasn't going to be blindly tricked, like Ryker had done to me.

"There are more pleasurable ways to destroy you."

"Like rip my throat out?" I asked.

He growled under his breath. "Like thrusting you against that stone bench and taking every fucking inch of your body, princess." He breathed deeply in my ear, and I shuddered. "Like spreading your legs and enjoying *my* fucking break- fast." He brushed his nose against my jaw. "Like sinking my teeth into your neck and marking you."

My heart raced at the thought.

Marking me? Marking me? No.

He shouldn't even suggest such a thing. Maybe he wanted to because it would hurt Roman for taking away his mate. A mate for a mate, just like an eye for an eye, the same side of the coin.

No, my wolf said, *he doesn't want to hurt Roman. He wants us. He's always wanted us.*

I thrust him away from me, my mind fuzzy with something that seemed like memories of us together at some point.

We don't want him, I said to my wolf, but it was a lie. *We never have.*

Suddenly, the sky darkened for a moment, and a bright ball of white light floated down from the sky, slowly transforming into a humanlike woman. My breath caught in the back of my throat at the way her brown curls drifted in the wind, the way her piercing blue eyes could see right through me, and the way soft white light radiated off her being.

The Moon Goddess.

She floated in the air above us and stared down at the entire estate. "Children," she said, angelic voice delicate yet stoic. "Thank you for attending my celebration for you and your wonderful abilities. Born under the Wolf Moon, you all hold a special place in my heart. I have put you through hard times to make you stronger and have given you the power to protect others when they're not strong enough to protect themselves.

"Today, tomorrow, and Sunday are days to celebrate you. One weekend, out of the many, when you have time for yourself, when divine law kicks into place and you can rest and rejuvenate ... so please, please do so. I look forward to chatting with you all soon."

After she descended onto the ground somewhere in the forest, I stood there, shocked. Rumor had had it that she'd be here. I just ... I hadn't known what I expected her to be like. I had only ever dreamed of meeting her one day, and that day had finally come.

The Moon Goddess herself—not the first divine wolves—was celebrating with us, and I had so many questions that I needed answered.

"Stay away from me," I said through my teeth at Kylo.

Then, I hurried through the garden toward the rest of the warriors and to our Moon Goddess.

He chuckled behind me, his ravishing voice drifting through the garden. "It's always you who finds me, Isabella."

CHAPTER 15

ISABELLA

*A*fter managing to avoid Kylo for the rest of Friday, I sat with a handful of the other warriors around a blazing bonfire on Saturday night. I hadn't even gotten a chance to talk to the Moon Goddess yesterday, as too many others had had her attention and I'd wanted to keep major distance from that cruel alpha who kept giving me those *eyes* from across the tulip garden.

"My wolf has been on edge lately," Darnell, a Wolf Moon warrior, said, scruffing his boot against the dirt. An agonizing frown was splayed across his face, and he choked back some whimpers. "The anniversary of my family's death is approaching."

I glanced from him to Kylo, who placed a sympathetic hand on Darnell's shoulder. Kylo looked my way, and I turned back to the fire with a frown. There were so many hard stories that I had listened to for the past hour and a half. Warriors spoke of the hardest, most demanding battles in and out of the forest. Some were physical, but most were mental wars.

"Humans killed them during the full moon, hunted us like it was a fucking game that night ..." Darnell continued, shaking his head. "I lost my mate and my babies." He let out a quiet sob. "Twin boys. They were only seven months."

I closed my eyes as a tear slid down my cheek. Thank the Goddess I didn't have a harrowing story like that. If Mom, Dad, or Roman died, I wouldn't be able to deal with it. It was hard enough that Luna Raya had been killed by a group of filthy rogues.

After Darnell finished, another warrior wolf named Connor looked over at Kylo. "What's your story?"

Almost unintentionally, I leaned forward and directed all my attention to Kylo. Maybe this would give me insight on what had happened between him and Roman that made them hate each other. Sure, Roman had taken his mate, but there must've been a reason why, right?

Kylo stared into the fire. "Seven years ago, I killed my father for raping a woman who was supposed to be his ally." He didn't look up, didn't shudder in disgust, didn't show even an ounce of emotion, except his eyes glistened with tears.

Kylo had killed his own father?

Strong male, my wolf said. *Protective partner.*

"At one point, I had looked up to him," Kylo continued with torment in every word. "I thought the way he treated my mother was how every man treated his mate ..." He parted his lips and then pressed them back together, as if he had changed his mind and didn't want to speak about the horrors he'd faced as a child.

Jazmine, another warrior, nudged him. "Go on. Nobody here will judge you."

Kylo took a deep breath and clenched his jaw. "He called

her a whore, a bitch, a slut, any name in the fucking book. He treated her like shit. And for the longest time, I treated my mate like that. She was young and impressionable, not even eighteen. I thought that was what men did, and then she left me. Around the same time, I found out that my dad had raped Alpha Roman's mom, and I lost it."

My eyes widened, pure shock darting through my body.

Oh my fucking Goddess.

Kylo's dad had raped Luna Raya.

A tear slid down Kylo's cheek as his lip twitched. Even from feet away, I felt every ounce of the insurmountable pain weighing on his shoulders at the loss of a mate and the knowledge of his once-poor character. This must've been why Roman had wanted to keep me from Kylo.

Kylo paused for a few moments, pressed his lips together, and stood. "That's all."

When Jazmine started to tell her story, I couldn't listen. My mind was too caught up with Kylo. He had killed his own father, driven away his mate, and been holding back all this shame.

Walking back into the forest alone, Kylo left us.

Follow him, my wolf said. *He is hurting.*

Jazmine looked between us and gave me that *it's okay to go comfort him* look. I smiled at her, nodded, and followed after Kylo through the woods and into the garden. Moonlight bounced off the pink petals, giving the estate a rosy glow.

"Kylo," I called. "Kylo, wait." I grabbed his wrist and pulled him back. "Stop, please."

Though I didn't expect him to stop for me, he paused and looked down at me with hurt in his brown eyes. I had never seen him look so vulnerable and so utterly broken. He was always Kylo, the sexy, strapping alpha who wanted me.

"I'm sorry I didn't tell you sooner. I didn't want to admit it aloud." He sat down on a stone bench. "I'm sorry I couldn't protect your pack from the rogue attack that killed Roman's parents. If I hadn't been so angry with my father and my mother for not telling me about it sooner, I would've been there to stop it. Your luna would still be alive."

"It's not your fault," I said, sitting down next to him and placing my hand on his knee. "It was the rogues who killed her. Nobody could've known that they were going to attack."

"But still …" His voice was quiet. "I would've been there."

After a few moments of silence, Kylo bumped his knee against mine and gazed out at the thousands of tulips. "You scare me," he said quietly over the slight hum of the warriors at the waterfall. "Every time I think about you, I feel the same intense desire for you that I felt with Scarlett. My wolf and I have grown, but I'm still terrified that I'm going to hurt you like I hurt her." He rested his forearms on his knees and clenched his fists. "I want to stay away, but I can't."

I scooted closer to him until our thighs brushed. "Why can't you stay away?" I whispered.

"Because, though I don't like that you're part of the Lycans, I value your strength and your commitment to making this world a better and safer place." He softly shook his head and grabbed my fingers, intertwining them with his.

The moonlight bounced off of his beautiful brown eyes, and all I wanted was to run my fingers up his neck and draw him closer to me.

But I resisted.

"I want you," he said as his sweet pine scent drifted through my nostrils. He moved closer to me, his face inches from mine, and tucked a strand of my hair behind my ear. "And I don't know why."

Giving in to my wolf, I rested my forehead against his. "What are you doing to me?" I asked, placing my fingers against his neck. Fuck staying away from him. I wanted him closer. So much closer.

He grasped the sides of my face, his thumbs brushing against my jawbones. Foreign butterflies fluttered through my stomach, up my torso, down my arms and legs, until my entire body tingled. I hadn't felt like this since Roman became my mate.

"Goddess, Isabella," he said, lifting my jaw. "I can't stay away from you any longer."

Tilting his head to the side, he leaned in slowly. I dug my nails into my palms and told myself that I couldn't betray Roman like this. Yet my wolf kept calling out for his wolf, begging me to let her feel his lips on hers again.

Again.

As if it had happened before in a past life.

When his lips were millimeters from mine, I purred. Not my wolf. Me.

Before he could even kiss me, he shuddered at the sound, his whole body shaking in pleasure. I could feel his wolf just underneath the surface, desperately clawing to get out, wanting to see me.

The mate's necklace that Roman had given me shifted on my neck, and I froze. This was wrong. What was my wolf thinking? What was I thinking? I shouldn't be here. This shouldn't be happening.

Kylo leaned closer to me, about to kiss me, when I turned my head. He placed his lips on my right cheek, just the mere feeling making me shiver in delight. I didn't know why I was reacting so strongly to him; I couldn't understand it. Why did I want something sinister? He wasn't my mate.

After letting his lips linger on my skin, Kylo swore under his breath and pulled away. We stared at each other in silence, the only sound coming from the faint music at the party by the lake. For a few moments, his eyes shifting back and forth between his wolf and his human, then Kylo finally glanced away.

I looked down at my feet and hugged my arms around my body, guilt washing over me like a tsunami. No matter how hard I tried, this feeling was just getting stronger. And now, I knew that it was more than just lust between us.

My wolf really, truly craved a connection with him.

"We can't do this anymore," I said. "I can't go behind Roman's back. I can't keep lying to Roman or to myself like this. We are wrong."

He stayed quiet. "What're you lying to yourself about?"

Goddess, I hated saying it. I hated *thinking* it.

"I like you," I whispered, grasping his hand. "I like you so fucking much, and I don't know how to make it stop."

"Why make it stop?" When he leaned closer, my wolf began to purr again. "All I know is that I haven't been able to get you out of my mind. Every time I close my eyes. Every time I go for a run. Every time I fucking breathe, Isabella. It's you."

I grasped his hands and stared into his brown eyes. "Because I have Roman."

Howls from other wolves echoed through the garden.

I stood up. "I need this to stop, Kylo. I need to find out why I feel this way for you." I led him in the direction of the waterfall, following the light to the Moon Goddess. "The Moon Goddess will help us understand."

The Moon Goddess stood at the edge of the waterfall, watching the Wolf Moon warriors splash around in the water. Though it was dark outside, she was bright enough to light the entire forest. With piercing blue eyes and curls that blew softly behind her, she glanced over at us and smiled.

"Isabella and Kylo," she said. "Are you ready to talk?"

I furrowed my brows. "You've been waiting for us?"

She laughed, her voice getting lost in the wind, and placed down a glass of white wine with moonflower sap. "Only since the weekend started," she said playfully. "You two are so aggravating to watch, on and off and on and off with all the flirting."

Kylo looked at me with one brow cocked and squeezed my hand. I hadn't let go of it yet.

After ushering us back toward the garden where it was more private, she said, "My dears, the Sky and I have had bets on how you two would end up. It's such a blessing to see you together again."

Again.

What did again mean?

We followed her through the gardens, letting her light our path.

And why would she have bets on us? Shouldn't she want us to be with our mates—the wolves who she'd assigned us to be together with forever?

She sat down on a stone bench, admiring her light as it bounced off of the tulips. "Now, what is it exactly that you want to know? Everything? Specific oddities maybe?"

Kylo squeezed my hand tighter, and I dropped his. It felt so wrong, yet the whole time, I had been gravitating toward him. The pull was becoming unbearably strong.

"I don't want to feel this connection with Kylo anymore," I blurted.

We do, my wolf said. *We love him.*

No. We don't.

We love Kylo. Kylo was our first love.

Stop it.

Kylo will always be our love.

I pressed my lips together, trying to get my wolf's thoughts out of my mind. It wasn't true. I didn't love him. He wasn't my first love. He wasn't even in love with me. My wolf was speaking utter nonsense.

"Oh, honey …" She stood up and brushed her knuckles against my cheek, making my skin tingle. "This connection will never go away. You are bound by my power, have been for thousands and thousands of years."

My heart raced. *Our first love.*

"How?" Kylo asked. "Are we mates?"

She chuckled. "No."

"Connected by the Wolf Moon?" I offered.

She arched a brow. "Do you feel this connection with anyone else here?"

"Then, what is it?" I asked, my fingers brushing against his fingers once more.

After pausing for a few moments, she smiled. "You two are connected because you're going to save the werewolf species from the war that lies ahead of you. There is a darkness coming, a darkness that I can't stop. It does not allow for divine intervention, and if it did … well, my powers alone are far too weak."

She brushed her fingers against the Lycan tattoo on the center of my back. "You two are my strongest warriors. You two have positioned yourselves in the best ways possible for the journey ahead. For you, Isabella, you have the Lycans." She gazed at Kylo, and I watched her light dance in his eyes. "For you, Kylo, you have this."

She held out her hand, and the flower that could kill any Wolf Moon warrior within seconds appeared in a small jar. He cautiously took it from her.

"The Wolf's Flower has been prophesied by many to bring an end to the darkness."

So many questions buzzed around my mind. Which darkness? What would it look like? Why were we the only ones who could stop it?

But me being me, I asked, "So, that's why I'm attracted to him? Because we're going to save the world?"

Placing her hands on each of our shoulders, she shook her head. "Not entirely. I have nothing to do with that desire of yours to let Kylo have you. Though mates are the most sacred connections that I can forge, your connection"—she gazed between us—"far surpasses that."

Kylo brushed his fingers against mine again, sending sparks up my arms. What she was saying didn't make sense to me. I wanted my mate to be my only connection, not someone else.

We want Kylo and Roman, my greedy little wolf said.

"I will not step between you because true love is out of my hands."

I stared at the Moon Goddess, just blinking and trying to understand what she had just said. "Are you saying that even if I reject Kylo and vow to never see him again, I'll still have feelings for him?"

"Correct."

"Aren't you the Moon Goddess? Can't you—"

Kylo placed a hand on my waist, rubbing small, circles on my skin to calm me.

"Sorry," I said.

"It's okay, my child. I know you're confused. Let me explain." She smiled. "The only time I have seen a connection like yours is between the divine wolves—my first creations and the strongest creatures to ever live. They died millennia ago, but their souls have—what you would call—free will. They have reincarnated into the strongest werewolf bodies over and over for the past seven thousand years and appear only when they sense danger is arising. Together, they defend the world against it, and then they die." She brushed her fingers against both of our cheeks, staring between us.

"And they have chosen you two, my children, to defeat the darkness that lies before us."

"That means that …"

She nodded her head. "That you are the divine wolves."

The divine wolves? The divine fucking wolves?

I stepped back and shook my head, tears filling my eyes. Everything that Roman and I had been through … had it all been for nothing? Had we fought and nearly broken up and gotten back together just to lose our connection? Or were we always fated to fall apart? What was going to happen to us?

Kylo had the same shocked expression written all over his face.

I wrapped my arms around myself. "Did you know who we were meant to be when choosing us to have different mates?" I asked, anger boiling inside of me because Roman was at the pack house, waiting for me to come home, alone. But after tonight, I would be coming home with Kylo, the man Roman hated the most, the man whose father had raped his mother.

He would hate me for this.

He would lose it.

He would hurt so fucking bad.

The Moon Goddess shook her head. "If I had known that the divine wolves would choose your bodies, I would have chosen you as mates." She reached out to grab my hand. "They are powerful creatures—almost as powerful as I am—and have their own liberty to so as they please. After defeating the last danger, they disappeared for hundreds of years. I never thought they'd return. After the last time, I thought they were gone for good."

After pushing away a stray tear, she cupped our faces and smiled so softly. "I never thought that I would see either of you again," she said.

My wolf howled inside of me and curled into her

embrace, acknowledging her as our creator, as our first mother, as our one true goddess.

More tears fell from her eyes, and I had the urge to comfort her. But she stepped away from us and gazed between Kylo and me. Kylo smiled at me, as if he felt the connection, too, but I didn't smile back.

"What's wrong?" he asked, brows knitting.

All my wolf wanted was to run into his arms and to tell him that nothing was wrong now that we had found each other. But something was wrong. Something was terribly wrong.

"Roman," I whispered. I brushed my fingers against my mate's necklace and clutched it in my hand like it was my most valuable possession—because it was. Roman meant more to me than all of this, than being a Lycan, than seeing the Moon Goddess, than finding out the truth.

But there was no denying the fact that there was something between Kylo and me.

"What's going to happen with Roman? Do I have to stop loving him? Do I have to … *reject* him?" I asked, barely able to get the word out. The thought of hurting Roman was pure torture. I loved him more than I loved myself even though it might not seem like it sometimes.

Kylo frowned.

How could I choose between my fated mate and my other half?

The Moon Goddess stepped forward. "Not unless you want to reject hi—"

"No, I don't ever want to reject him."

"You can still be with him," she confirmed. "In fact, each of you can still be with your mate—"

She stopped herself and glanced at Kylo with a grievous expression.

Kylo stared down at his feet, his pain so strong that my

wolf physically hurt from it. It was pain that lingered from his mate's heartbreak, from watching his mate with Roman, from treating her poorly all these years.

After swallowing hard, the Moon Goddess looked directly at me. "You can still have Roman as your mate, Isabella. And Kylo may choose what he would like me to do for him since he now knows about the connection between you two."

Kylo parted his lips and then pressed them back together. "I can ... choose?"

"If you'd like a second-chance mate, if you'd like to be mateless, if you'd like to continue your life with your other half, you may choose," she said.

For a moment, he glanced between us, and then he turned away. I didn't know what I wanted him to say. Maybe I wanted him to choose me. Maybe I wanted him to choose Scarlett to get her out of Roman's hair. Maybe I wanted him to be happy, and if that meant choosing someone else, then he would get another mate.

"I want Isabella to be happy," Kylo said finally.

"Well," the Moon Goddess said, "I will leave you to be happy together. You have one more day here by yourselves. Enjoy it."

CHAPTER 16

KYLO

When the Moon Goddess left the garden, it was past three a.m. Flames from the bonfire nearly licked the bottoms of branches, other wolves were returning to their cabins for the night, and Isabella walked with me through the hundreds of flowers with the same shocked expression that I must be wearing.

My mother had only ever told myths of the first two divine wolves, their strength comparable to the gods and the somber stories of their departure from this world. Two wolves who had been destined to be together, forced apart by evil and death.

I'd never thought it was real.

Before we reached Isabella's cabin, I grabbed her hand and tugged her in the direction of the waterfall. Tonight was the first night we could truly spend together. And after what the Moon Goddess had told us, I wasn't going to waste it.

"Kylo," she said, pulling on my arm. If she really wanted to pull out of my grip, she could. But she didn't. "Kylo, I can't."

"Let me spend some time with you before we leave tomorrow." I squeezed her hand harder, my wolf loving the feeling of her skin on mine, and continued toward the lake. "I don't know when or if Roman will ever let me."

When we reached the waterfall, I tugged my shirt and pants off. My lips curled into a smile as she glanced down my body for a moment. I dived into the lake, the cold water waking up my senses.

This is our only chance to see our love, our first, my wolf said to me. *Don't mess this up.*

When I came up for air, I swam back toward the edge. "Come join me."

Isabella crossed her arms over her chest and gnawed on the inside of her lip. Guilt plagued her heart—my wolf could feel it surging through her, her loyalty to Roman holding her back from us.

Reassure her, my wolf said, desperate to have her in his arms.

"Please," I whispered, holding out my hand. "I won't do anything to you."

She stared, her eyes flickering to her wolf's gold color. After unfolding her arms, she peeled off her clothes and jumped into the water with me. White bubbles drifted to the top of the water a few feet away, frothing under some lily pads.

Although she swam closer to me, she kept her distance.

Those eyes and her scent and my wolf were a wicked mix.

I snatched her wrist and pulled her to my chest, the water rippling between us. As I swam next to her, I took it all in for the first time. Every single strand of gold in her eyes. How her hair glimmered under the moon. The intensity surged through my body when she touched me.

93

All I wanted to do was pull her closer and closer, but she would stop me.

Instead, I rested my forehead against hers and listened to her uneven breaths and the quick pace of her heart until she finally said, "What are you going to do?"

I furrowed my brows. "What do you mean?"

She stared at me for a bit and chewed on her bottom lip. "What are you going to do about … your mate?"

My breath caught in the back of my throat, and I didn't know what she wanted me to say. My wolf wanted to love her. All this time, he had been keeping it to himself because he didn't want things to go even further south with Roman and Isabella. But now … I couldn't stop thinking about what a life could look like with her.

Grasping her chin, I brought her closer to me and let my nose brush against hers. "I told the Moon Goddess that I wanted to make you happy," I said honestly.

But Roman was too controlling, too alpha to even share her with me. It broke my heart.

I would never truly get Isabella to myself.

She closed her big blue eyes and inhaled deeply. When she reopened her eyes, they were a mess of gold and blue, the strands tangled together, her and her wolf one. "Don't you want a mate? Don't you wish that you can love someone again? Don't you think that—"

Without thinking, I pressed my lips to hers. My wolf took control of me as my fingers curled into her waist to bring her closer to me. I was hungry and desperate to touch her again. It felt like it had been centuries since I had last tasted her.

She placed her hands on my chest and softly kissed me back. Tingles ran up and down my spine. I hadn't experienced something so intense for such a long time, maybe never in this lifetime.

After a few moments, I pulled away and asked, "What did you feel?"

A look of pure confusion washed over her face. "I love Roman. I love Roman so much."

Ache. Heartbreak. Uncertainty. Did she not feel what I felt?

"That's not what I asked," I said. I lifted her chin, so her eyes met mine. "How did that kiss make you feel?"

"I'm not supposed to feel this," she said, fingers digging into my chest. "I'm not."

"Be honest with yourself, princess."

She hesitantly wrapped her arms around my shoulders. "I liked it," she whispered.

"Okay," I said, my mind made up.

"Okay?" she asked. "What does that mean?"

"It means that I'm not going to ask for another mate. I don't need one."

"Kylo, we can't be—"

"I know that you have Roman and that we have other things going on right now. I don't need another woman." I straightened out my shoulders. I hadn't needed another mate for years now. "And besides, I can control myself around you."

She arched a brow. "Is that so?"

I wrapped my arms around her waist and pulled her toward the waterfall. "Sometimes."

CHAPTER 17

ROMAN

$\mathcal{M}$y mate mark sizzled, fucking hissing in my ear like a venomous serpent warning me that my mate was with another man. It was three thirty a.m., and the pain hadn't stopped for at least half an hour. I paced around my dark room with my hand against my skin, hoping to cool it off.

Isabella must've been with Kylo, doing goddess knew what with him.

Flirting? Kissing? Fucking for all I knew.

I slammed my fist against the wall in our bedroom, causing the moonflowers on our windowsill to tremble slightly. The light emitting off them was dimmer compared to the nights Isabella stayed here with me.

How could Isabella believe all of Kylo's blatant lies? How could she think there was something between them when I was her mate? How could I let him slowly drag her away from me?

When I had been growing up, Mom had always told me that I needed to protect my mate from all the evils of the world. But how could I protect someone who was not only stronger than me, but defiant too? It seemed like everyone I ever loved was being taken away from me.

Mom had been killed by rogues. Dad had died minutes later. Then, Jane had mated with Raj.

Now, my own mate had a *connection* with my ex–best friend, who *conveniently* had the Wolf's Flower that could kill Isabella and eliminate the Lycans for good. It must've been his fucking plan all along.

My phone buzzed, and I hurried over to it, hoping that it was Isabella.

Unknown Number: I have information about the Wolf's Flower.

Furrowing my brows, I stared down at the phone.

Me: Who's this?

Unknown Number: Romie, there are only a few people who know about the Wolf's Flower and your mate. ;)

I rolled my eyes and collapsed onto the bed with my head in my hands. Of course it was fucking Scarlett. She had an almost-humorous way of weaseling into any drama that she could find. And if the rumors of her pack being in havoc were true, she was desperate for safety. She might have solid information for me.

Suddenly, Vanessa barged into the room without knocking. "Don't answer it, Roman."

I stared at her with wide eyes. "What're you doing here?"

She snatched my phone and pushed it into her back jeans pocket. "I overheard Scarlett talking about contacting you to get back together at The Night Raider's Café. Don't fall into her trap and hurt Isabella," she said, voice soft and full of worry.

Vanessa had never cared so much about Isabella before

she became a Lycan. It didn't add up that Vanessa wanted to be close friends with her now and neither did Scarlett wanting to get back together. I had told her no once, and my answer wouldn't ever change.

"Give me my phone back," I said through clenched teeth.

Scarlett could have information about when Kylo would use the flower to kill Isabe—

I stopped mid-thought because I sounded so stupid. Scarlett was selfish. She didn't care who lived and who died, who thrived and who hurt. She had betrayed her own mate and wouldn't think twice about betraying me for any reason.

This message was a trap. It had to be.

Vanessa crossed her arms over her chest. "No, I'll deal with Scarlett myself." She stepped toward me in a threatening manner and pointed a sharp, manicured finger at me. "I know you were listening to our conversation the other night. You know how much Isabella loves you. Don't make her not trust you by texting Scarlett."

"Why're you so obsessed with her?" I asked, blowing out a breath and sitting back down on the bed.

As much as I hated to admit it, Vanessa was right. Whatever was between Isabella and Kylo would hopefully be sorted out this weekend. And Isabella would tell me everything.

My mark burned hotter, and I clutched it in my hand.

She had better.

Vanessa crossed her arms over her chest. "Because she's my friend."

"You hated her in high school."

For the first time *ever*, Vanessa growled at me. "Because I fucking like her, Roman, okay? Goddess, why do you ask so many questions?" Almost as soon as the words left her lips, her eyes widened. She slapped a hand over her mouth.

Vanessa liked Isabella? Was that why she had made fun of

her every day, why she had flirted endlessly with any guy Isabella showed attention to in high school—to get her attention?

"You know what? I don't care that you know. I just want Isabella to be happy." Vanessa dropped her hand. "Make sure you appreciate her and her strength, or someone else will," she threatened and walked out.

CHAPTER 18

ISABELLA

*S*oft orange sunlight flooded around tree branches, bounced off of the small lake near the rushing waterfall, and reflected right onto my closed eyes. I grumbled to myself and turned onto my side, curling into Roman's muscular chest to hide from the sun.

With his strong arms around me and his fingers gently caressing my back, he pulled me closer and breathed against my neck. I tugged myself even closer to his naked chest and inhaled his pine scent. *So good. He smelled so damn good.*

Like I did every morning, I reached to grasp his mate's necklace, but it wasn't there.

His neck was bare. Completely bare. Without a mate's necklace and without a mark.

I snapped my eyes open and stared at Kylo, who shifted in the sand to lie on his stomach and let his toes dip into the rippling lake. Within an instant, I scrambled away from him and clutched the closest piece of damp clothing I could find, pulling it onto my body to hide myself.

Oh Moon Goddess. No. No. No. No. No. No. No.

The last thing I remembered was staring up at the stars with him and wondering how we were the two most sacred and admired divine wolves. We must've just fallen asleep. No sex. Thankfully, no sex. That kiss last night was enough for this entire weekend.

More, my wolf purred. *We need another kiss.*

"Kylo!" I whisper-yelled, shoving his muscular shoulder. "Wake up!"

After mumbling to himself, he slowly opened his tired eyes to gaze up at me. Turning onto his back, he lay there naked in all of his glory, not caring for a single moment that all his junk was out for everyone to see.

Before I could react, he grabbed my wrist and pulled me back down to his chest. "I've never woken up with you before," he said softly against my jaw. He took a deep breath, his chest rising and falling. "I haven't woken up next to a woman in years."

"Kylo, please."

I shifted in his arms, but he held me closer. "Let me enjoy you, Isabella. I want to savor this moment and all the little things that come along with you in the morning. I don't know when Roman will let me see you again."

My body relaxed against him, and I closed my eyes. *Savor the moment because we might not get another one.* It felt so wrong, but my wolf kept purring, and I wanted to keep her content. She had wanted this for so long.

"Tell me one thing that makes you happy," he said after moments of silence.

Roman, I thought, *and you.*

Chest tightening, I smiled and brushed some hair from his forehead. "I love moonflowers. We have tons of them in pots on our windowsill. They glow at all hours of the night," I turned onto my back and grinned even harder. "And sometimes, I catch Roman smiling at them."

Kylo curled his fingers into my side, making me turn back to him. "I have a garden of them in my pack. I planted them for Luna Raya after she died. She loved them, too, didn't she?"

My heart warmed, and I nodded. "She did," I whispered.

Just as Kylo was about to speak, wolves howled in the distance.

Kylo grabbed my hand and tugged me to my feet. "Morning departure meeting with the Moon Goddess," he said, grabbing his dirty shirt from the sand. "We can't be late."

After a short stroll to the garden under chirping and whistling bluebirds, we reached the group of warriors huddled around the Moon Goddess. She stood among them, skin softer and less bright than last night, and glanced around until she met our gazes. We stood near the back with our shoulders brushing against each other—my need to be near him intensifying every moment—and listened to her speak about the darkness that would soon plague the entire world if we didn't stop it.

"Havoc will spread and threaten the werewolf race faster than any epidemic, sickness, or mania has ever unraveled. It won't be anything like you have seen in your lifetimes. People will die." She looked at us. "People you love will die."

When the warriors broke out into a fit of whispers and murmurs, she held up her hand to quiet everyone down. "Please, stay calm and ask your questions."

"What is this darkness?" someone in the crowd asked.

"His name is Dolus, God of Corruption. While I'm fighting him in the divine sphere, he has warriors on the ground who are slowly trying to corrupt people's minds."

She gestured to me. "Ryker, the previous leader of the Lycans, was one of those he had manipulated. After he marked Michelle, he was vulnerable and an easy target to taint."

Ryker? That man had been so hard to take down. If there were more people like that ...

"There are others around that I'm sure you've been in contact with. I can't tell you exactly who he has already corrupted because corruption comes in many forms that are similar to the way mortals normally act. Some people are devious, envious, or simply evil."

Clouds drifted over the sun, barring any light, except hers.

She paused and shook her head, a somber expression crossing her face. "I am doing everything I can, but I can't do it all. Every time he corrupts a mind, he becomes stronger and harder to hold back. Once he corrupts thirty percent of the population, I won't be able to hold him back any longer. He will come to this beautiful earth and bring hell upon it. I need your help to save our species from corruption."

More whispers broke out among the crowd, yet this time, it wasn't fear of the unknown plaguing everyone's words. It was the sense of protection, power, want, and need to save our species. Warriors stood taller, canines emerged from under their lips, and nails lengthened into their claws.

The Wolf Moon warriors were ready to fight.

"You will be led by the two reincarnated divine wolves. Please, do as they say, as they hold the knowledge of seven thousand years of war in their minds and in their muscles." She smiled at us. "Isabella and Kylo will lead you to victory."

When everyone turned toward us, Kylo awkwardly raised a hand, and I gulped nervously.

While the Lycans depended on me to make the right decisions to protect people from rogues, I now had to make decisions that would affect the survival of our species. It was terrifying.

"You are dismissed," the Moon Goddess said. "Make me proud."

After she disappeared into the woods, Kylo and I stayed behind until everyone left the estate. There were so many warriors on our side, who had so much collective experience. We had the control, and we would destroy whatever got in our way.

Once the last warrior, Darnell, left, Kylo grabbed my hand and led me to the exit. Heart pounding inside my chest, I intertwined my fingers with his. Whether we had been lovers in a past life, friends in others, or sworn enemies—like Roman wanted to be in this life—we had to be on one team to defeat corruption.

"I need to tell Roman about us," I said, stepping on the other side of the stone gates. "But I need you to be there when I do. He needs to understand what you are to me and that we can't fight anymore. Please warn your pack, get everything you need in order, and come to Roman's pack tonight."

He cupped my face in his hands and brushed his thumbs against my cheeks. "Whatever you need, Isabella." He placed his lips on my cheek, shifted into his wolf, and disappeared into the forest.

When I arrived at our pack, Roman was waiting at the border for me with dark circles under his eyes, a weak smile on his face, and a moonflower in his hand. "Isabella," he whispered, handing me the flower and studying every inch of my body as if it were the first time he had ever seen it. He brushed his knuckles across my cheek and smiled down at me. "My dear Isabella."

After inhaling deeply, he tensed for a brief moment—probably smelling Kylo on me—and then relaxed as much as he could. I wrapped my arms around his shoulders and pulled him into a hug, needing him close. As I rested my face against his chest, right above the heart that beat for me, I slumped my shoulders forward and let a tear fall down my cheek.

It had only been two days. We had been apart for longer. But I had never been this far from him—mentally or emotionally.

Being in his arms again felt better than I'd imagined it would.

I grabbed his hand and tugged him toward the pack house. While Kylo might've been my wolf's first love, Roman was mine. We were going to talk, but I first wanted to show him that he was the only person *I* needed.

Leading him up to our bedroom, I pushed him onto the bed, crawled onto him, and kissed him hard on the lips. Since we had been children chasing each other around his back-yard and drawing little pictures of warrior wolves with red crayons on the walls, Roman had been everything to me.

He always would.

Roman rolled on top of me, kissed down my neck to his mark, and slowly peeled off our clothes. The moment wasn't rushed, but passionately slow. He scooted between my legs, smiled down at me, and tucked some hair behind my ear.

"I'm ready for you to lead us," he said, kissing my mark. "I know that Kylo has given you more respect as a warrior than I ever have." He pecked my jaw and then pulled back and stared directly into my eyes. "But I want you to know that you're everything to me. You're strong and powerful and such a wonderful leader." He brushed his fingers against my lips. "I hope that I'm not too late."

All those familiar little butterflies fluttered around in my stomach. My heart swelled, and I felt like we were two stupid kids without a care in the world again, wanting to just love each other for who we were.

"You're not too late, Roman," I murmured against his lips. "I'm still yours." I pulled him down closer to me and brushed my nose against his, closing my eyes. "And you're still mine."

I just wanted to love him.

No more miscommunication. No more secrets. No more lies.

Curling a hand around the back of my neck, he pulled me closer and pressed his lips hard to mine, kissing me with everything he had. And when we were both breathless, he worked his way down my jaw, down my neck, down my chest and stomach until he reached my panties.

After looping two fingers inside the black material, he peeled them off of me and admired every inch of my legs as they slid down them. I squirmed under his gaze, aching. He drew his nose down the inside of my right thigh until he met my core. He spread my legs apart and pressed his hot mouth onto my clit.

Instead of squirming around and back-talking like I usually did, I lay there and enjoyed it.

My back arched. My fingers curled into his hair. My eyes stayed on his as he loved me.

"I love you, Isabella," he murmured against me.

Overcome with so much raw emotion, I couldn't hold back the tears that formed in my eyes. I curled my fingers into his shoulder and relaxed further into the mattress. He continued to lap at my clit, his tongue flicking back and forth over it.

"I never want to stop loving you," he said.

A tear rolled down my cheek. Despite everything that we had faced and everything that we *would* face together, I loved this man, and I would never stop loving him either. He would be with me until the day I died.

Slowly kissing his way back up my stomach, he left a trail of tingles on my body. He brushed his fingers oh-so softly against my cheek to push away a single tear. But it only made more of them fall.

When he pressed his lips to mine, he pushed himself into me. My core tightened around his cock, shaping to him naturally. He slowly pumped into me while whispering soft, calming *I love you*s into my ear.

"My dear Isabella," he murmured against me, resting his forehead against mine and creating soothing patterns around my nipple with his fingers, "I want you to come."

I furrowed my brows, whimpering.

"Can you do that for me?"

I nodded, my heart pounding. "Yes, Roman."

He brushed two fingers against my clit and rubbed me in small circles. "Come for me."

Clenching on his cock, I stared up at him through teary eyes and let my legs tremble around him as I came undone for him.

CHAPTER 19

ROMAN

*A*fter I made love to Isabella, she lay on my chest, drew circles around on my abdomen, and told me that Kylo was coming over tonight to talk. I tensed underneath her and inhaled his scent, which lingered in her hair.

She had been with him this weekend—the *entire* weekend.

From the moment I had first smelled him on her—at the Lycans' pack house—I had known that something was going on between them. I had known he'd try to hit on her or kill her with that flower even, but I just didn't want to think that Isabella could be swept away by him, especially after all we'd been through.

During the entire time we had been lying together tonight, she had cried so many tears. I had thought they were tears of joy and love and passion … but that evil, insecure part of me shouted that those were heartbroken tears. All I could think about was Isabella leaving me for him tonight, about her ripping off her mate's necklace and throwing it at me when he got here.

So many thoughts ran recklessly through my mind. I desperately needed to know what this goddess-damned connection was between them. All weekend, I had prepared myself for the worst—for her to reject me as her mate. My insecurities said that it was coming any day now. Rejecting me so she could be with Kylo, just like Scarlett had rejected Kylo to be with me.

Guards warned me that Kylo was here through the mind link. I scooped Isabella up in my arms, dressed her, and walked down the stairs to the front of the pack house with her small hand enveloped in mine.

I couldn't let her leave with him, and I wouldn't if that was what he was here for.

Kylo stood in the front yard, brown eyes lighting up when he saw her. She tightened her grip on my hand and refused to look me in the face, yet I saw the way her eyes sparkled almost as brightly as they did the night she had discovered we were mates.

My heart pounded inside my chest, canines emerging under my lips. This was it. I was going to lose her, too, like I had lost everyone else that I cared about. And when Kylo finally had her …

I shook my head, unsure of how that would play out.

If he wanted to kill her, he could've killed her with that flower this weekend. Yet he hadn't.

Instead of reaching for him like I'd thought she would, Isabella stepped away from both of us and cleared her throat, directing her attention toward me. "We need to tell you something."

Every ounce of pain rushing through her body raced through mine as well. I balled my hands into fists to keep my claws hidden. My wolf stayed on edge, glancing back and forth between Kylo and Isabella.

She squeezed her eyes shut and reopened them with tears. "Kylo and I—"

"Did you cheat on me?" I blurted out, wanting to put everything on the table.

Waiting another second would kill me.

"Roman, I—we … we didn't have sex, if that's what you're asking." Tears streamed down her blotchy red cheeks. "I have a connection with him." She curled her arms around herself to make herself smaller. "He's my wolf's first mate."

When the words came out of her mouth, I broke. Fiery agony spread through my body, as if every part of me had been doused in gasoline. I shook my head, not wanting to believe it. How could this be fucking true?

I was her mate. I had been made for her.

"Wh-what?" I asked so softly that I barely heard myself. "You two are mates?"

"This isn't me trying to get back at you for what you did with Scarlett, Roman," Kylo said, straightening himself out. Light from the moon glowed behind him, making his face dark and ominous. "I swear to the goddess that it isn't."

"What do you mean, you're fucking mates?" I growled, ignoring him.

The entire forest went silent, not even racoons scurrying up the trees or bats chirping.

"Not like us." Isabella placed her hands on my chest. Familiar tingles ran up and down my arms as she stepped closer to me. "Kylo and I have a different connection with our wolves." When she stopped, he nodded to her and urged her to continue. "Our wolves are divine, the first two wolves to ever bear the powers of shifting, reincarnated for thousands and thousands of years," she said to me. "And the Moon Goddess said that we need to save the world together."

I pulled myself away from her. I didn't like it. I didn't fucking like it at all.

Staring up at me with those big, beautiful, glossy eyes, her brows drawn slightly together, she frowned. "I'm sorry, Roman. I'm sorry for being so jealous about Scarlett when … when I couldn't stop feeling this way toward Kylo."

Kylo gazed at me with hurt in his eyes—the same hurt that I'd caused when I started dating his mate. Both of us had screwed up, but this was too far.

I loathed this more than the thought of her leaving me for him just because.

I ached to wrap my hands around his throat and squeeze hard until he crumpled beneath me. The thought of her wolf being in love with Kylo for thousands upon thousands of years made me feel like shit.

Did her wolf not love me? Did her wolf not purr for me every night we lay in bed together? Was it all just some put-on?

She grabbed my hand in one of hers and grasped my jaw in the other. "Roman, please say something," she pleaded, voice so soft and quiet. Every word she spoke was filled with hurt and despair.

I wanted to hate her wolf for this, but fuck, I loved her. I had loved her and her wolf since we were pups, play-fighting in the forest, since we sneaked into the cave and drew stupid little pictures on the walls for hours, since we used to run home when the fireflies went to bed and the sun started to rise above the trees.

After frowning down at my feet, I pulled myself away from her. "Why didn't you tell me that you felt this strongly about him sooner?" I asked, trying to keep myself under control and not turn her around, thrust her against the nearest tree, and claim what was *mine* in front of the man who was taking her away from me.

"I tried to ignore it," she whispered, clutching my hand tightly. "I tried to make our connection go away, but my wolf kept leading me back to him. All I've felt is so much guilt and sorrow and sadness because"—she hiccuped—"I love you so much and I don't want to lose you."

I swallowed all of my pain. "What if you lost me?"

More tears raced down her cheeks. "R-R-Rom ..." She couldn't even finish my name.

She ached on the inside; I could feel it. It was killing me.

But smelling him on her each night made me hurt worse.

When she grasped my hand again, I pulled it away from her. "Isabella," I said, lifting her chin so she'd look me right in my face. "What if you lost me? Tell me how you'd feel."

She squeezed her eyes closed and hugged her arms around her body.

"Open your eyes," I demanded. "Look at me when you say it."

After she opened her eyes, they shifted back and forth between gold and blue. "I ... I would feel so broken on the inside. I would feel so terrible. I would hate myself. You're all I know. You're all that I've *ever* known." She placed her hands on mine and held on tight. "I love you with everything that I have. I haven't taken my mate's necklace off of me since the moment you put it on me. I haven't loved another man like I love you."

Though my heart ached, I held back my tears. I wanted to cry so fucking hard because I loved her too fucking much. She could ruin me over and over and over, and I would still want to worship every inch of her body, mind, and soul.

"And what if you lost Kylo?" I asked, keeping my jaw clenched so she wouldn't see it tremble. Just asking her the question broke me because I already knew the answer, but I wasn't sure if I was ready for her to say it.

Kylo stared at her, brows furrowed, waiting for her to

respond. His reaction to her answer would be all I needed to know that this wasn't all some big act from him, that whatever was between them was true and not something he had told her to attract her.

Isabella parted her lips and then closed them.

I grasped her jaw a bit harder and nodded my head. "How would you feel, my dear Isabella? Truthfully?"

She closed her eyes for the briefest moment and then opened them back up. "My wolf would be heartbroken. She would be weak. She would hate me for pushing him away from her. She loves him."

"I didn't ask how your wolf would feel. I asked how you would."

She furrowed her brows again and frowned. "I would feel broken too."

CHAPTER 20

ISABELLA

roken. I would feel broken and incomplete without Kylo, and I hated it so much.

Roman gently grasped my face, brushing his thumbs across my cheeks. His eyes shifted between a hundred different shades of gold until they eventually settled on their rich hazel color. And all I could see within them was that same look of failure and sorrow I had seen in them when I told him I had to leave for the Lycans.

When he parted his lips, I braced myself for the harshest rejection that I would ever face. We were mates. He had marked me. I had marked him. We wore each other's mate's necklaces like they were a second skin. And I knew that he would tell me that he couldn't be with someone who would leave him for another man.

If he did that, I wouldn't even fight him about it. I deserved it. I was selfish for needing two mates.

"This is my worst fear," Roman finally said, looking at me

and then Kylo. "My own mate being taken away from me and putting herself into so much danger that I could lose her as she tries to save the world."

Kylo stepped forward. "I won't hurt her."

"Kylo, please," I whispered.

I didn't want anyone to start a fight. If Roman was going to reject me, I wanted him to just get it over with now. I couldn't handle all the damn anticipation of it.

Roman walked over to the bushes of moonflowers, brushing his fingers against the petals. "What did the Moon Goddess say to you about saving the world?" he asked instead of rejecting me straightaway. "What is coming?"

"It's not coming," Kylo said, clearing his throat. "Corruption is already here."

I gazed at Kylo, my heart pounding at the thought of a darkness plaguing our people. "There's a darkness in this world that is spreading among werewolves fairly quickly. His name is Dolus. He corrupts the minds of his victims, corrupts them to control them to enter the darkness. The Moon Goddess is currently holding him back, but once his corruption spreads to at least thirty percent of the population, he will truly be unleashed."

"Ryker?" he asked.

"Ryker was one of the corrupted."

After rocking back on his heels with his arms crossed over his chest, he turned away from me. "Who is at risk?"

I frowned at him and looked at my feet. At this particular moment, he could be someone at risk because he was hurting and weak. He could be corrupted because of my connection to Kylo.

When I didn't say anything, he grasped my wrist. "Me? I'm someone at risk, aren't I?"

I grasped his face and drew my thumbs against his cheekbones. "Your mind is strong, Roman. You're strong. So

strong. Yes, there is a chance that you could be corrupted …
but I won't let him hurt you—ever."

Kylo stepped forward and stared Roman directly in the
eyes. "Neither will I."

Roman clenched his jaw and then unclenched it. He
looked back at me and clutched my hand harder. A breeze
blew some strands of his light-brown hair across his forehead. "What do you have to do?" he asked.

"The Moon Goddess told me that I will need to use the
Lycans and Kylo needs to use the Wolf's Flower to defeat the
darkness. I'm expecting that it will be a difficult journey
because Dolus is a god, a deceptive one."

"So, we're going to war?" Roman asked.

"We're going to war," I confirmed.

Roman looked back at Kylo. "Isabella, I need to talk to
Kylo privately."

"Wait, you want me to leave?" I asked, gazing between the
two men and trying to figure out if they would kill each
other if I left.

While Roman was hyped up on adrenaline, he seemed
relatively calm—too calm.

"Okay. I'll go over to Vanessa's for tonight." I gnawed on
the inside of my lips. "Can … can I have a kiss good night?"

Roman grabbed my hips and drew me closer to him,
placing his lips on mine. It wasn't for long, just a few
moments, but it was filled with as much passion as the kiss
he had given me in bed earlier. "I'll text you when we're
finished."

After hesitantly nodding, I gathered some essentials from
our bedroom and left for Vanessa's. I wanted to stay behind,
to see what they were talking about, but I had to trust them
not to tear each other apart. They needed to get along—or at
least act as if they did—because the world was going to shit,
and I didn't know if we'd all survive it.

CHAPTER 21

KYLO

*R*oman popped the caps off two beers and handed me one. "Let's get one thing straight," he said, walking toward the blazing bonfire in his backyard. "We're not friends."

I sat on a damp log across from him and sipped the drink. "We don't have to be friends."

With his hand clasped hard around the bottle, he leaned forward toward the fire. "I don't accept this. I don't like this. I fucking *hate* this thing going on between you and my mate," he said, orange flames reflecting in his bitter gold eyes.

After taking another swing, I nodded. "I know you do."

"I fucked shit up too much and tried so hard to get Isabella back. I don't plan on losing her again." He tipped his drink back. "I *will not* lose her again."

Not knowing what the hell he wanted me to say, I decided on the truth. "Well, I like her."

There had been far too many lies barked between our

younger selves. We were both men now. Roman might've had to mature faster, but he had a long way to go to really understand what love was and what love wasn't, how he should act in a relationship with his mate and how he shouldn't act.

"You *love* her," Roman corrected, like he had been thinking about those words for so long that they turned sour on his tongue. "You love what is mine, just like I loved what was yours."

The fire crackled.

I kicked my boot up on the log he sat on, dirt blowing in the slight breeze, and leaned forward. "Except you never loved Scarlett. You can tell Isabella that you did, but you never saw the real side of her. You wouldn't have loved the way that she screamed and cried and begged for me to love her when you found your mate. You wouldn't have loved the way she left you late at night to go off on her own adventures, deep into the woods with the rogues. You wouldn't have loved the way she told you that you were the most amazing person in the entire world and then left you crying in bed every night and wondering if you were enough. You wouldn't have loved the emotional damage that she would've caused you if you'd stayed with her long enough."

It had been difficult to see at the time, but Scarlette and I had both been abusive toward each other. Maybe that was why I had refused to be with anyone since her. I was scared that I would hurt another woman and that she would hurt me too.

Roman sipped his beer and sighed. "You're right. I probably wouldn't have."

In the past four years, that was the first bit of understanding we'd ever had.

"I really love Isabella," I said after another gulp.

She had faults. Everyone did. But she was better to me

than Scarlett ever had been. She was strong, confident, stoic almost. And something about her always made me smile.

"The way the moon bounces off her skin. The way her laugh echoes through the forest late at night."

"Her smile ... her fucking breathtaking smile." Roman stared into the fire, the corner of his lip curling up. "And her eyes filled with so much passion for the people and the things she loves the most."

"Her grace."

"Her willpower."

"Her dominance. Goddess, I love her dominance."

Roman chuckled. "You wouldn't like it in the bedroom."

"There's nothing wrong with a woman being dominant in the bedroom."

"Isabella isn't dominant in the bedroom. She'll get on your very last nerve." Roman smirked as he stared into the fire, looking as if he was lost in his own little world. "In the most fucked up, irresistible way possible." He paused, suddenly tense, and looked me directly in the eye. "When you were at the party, did you and she ..."

"No," I said honestly. "We didn't."

He covered his face with his hands and exhaled, shoulders slumping forward.

While I didn't know what to say, I knew that I had to apologize and clear the air between us—to get through this and to help him realize that Isabella needed me just as much as she needed him. We had once been best friends, and now, we were bitter enemies. It couldn't be like that anymore, no matter how much each of us wanted it.

"Listen, Roman." I placed my beer on the ground, rested my forearms on my knees, and leaned forward. "I'm sorry for not being here for you when your parents were killed. I could've tried to stop it, but I didn't. I handled the Scarlett situation in an immature way, and I truly apologize for everything that I have done and everything that my father did to you and your family."

Roman gazed up at me, grimacing slightly, and nodded. "I don't blame you for it." He paused. "I shouldn't have taken Scarlett from you. It was a shitty thing to do, especially to one of my best friends. I was angry and upset after finding out what happened to my mom."

"Scarlett is gone now." I shook my head. "We're both better off without her."

Another awkward silence fell upon us until Roman finally spoke up. "Isabella loves you," he said. "I can see it in her eyes and hear it in her voice." He looked at me. "And I need your word that you're going to do every-fucking-thing you can do to protect her, that you're willing to give your life to protect my Isabella as much as I am."

I looked him right in the eye. "I would die for her, Roman."

CHAPTER 22

ISABELLA

*L*ying on Vanessa's living room floor in one of her plush pink robes, I grabbed a strawberry from the bowl between us and stared up at the ceiling fan spinning in circles. All I could think about since the moment I'd arrived was Roman and Kylo, *alone*, at the pack house.

"So," Vanessa said, pouring herself some more white wine. Dressed in a silky black robe, she lay back down next to me and rested her head on my shoulder. "What's a secret that you've never told anyone, even Roman?"

The wine hit me hard, making me just a bit woozy. "I don't have many secrets."

She rolled onto her stomach. "Oh, come on. I'm sure that you have something."

"There's nothing." I rolled onto my tummy, too, and sipped my wine. "Noth-ing."

Vanessa curled a finger around a strand of my brown hair

and released it, watching it bounce. "Nothing?" she asked, kicking her legs back and forth. "I don't believe it."

"Okay, fine. But you can't tell anyone."

With wide eyes, she leaned forward. "Tell me!"

"I remember when Roman started dating Scarlett. He was thirteen, fourteen maybe. And I hated her, absolutely hated her—more than I hated you at the time. I hated her so much that I made Derek steal her purse and fart in it."

She burst out in laughter, tears streaming down her face. "Oh Goddess, you did not."

I clutched my stomach, bursting out in laughter at the memory. "She opened it up to get some of her cherry lip gloss and … and … oh my Goddess …" All I could remember was the pure look of terror on her face. "Derek and I watched from the trees and could smell it from there."

After wiping some tears from cheeks, she giggled some more. "Oh damn. I don't think I have anything that could beat that."

Taking another sip of my wine, I nudged her. "It doesn't have to be funny, just a secret."

"I …" she said, taking a deep breath. "I have a secret that I haven't told anyone really."

"Not even Jane?"

"Not even Jane."

"Well, go on. What is it?" I asked, kicking my legs back and forth in the air.

She parted her lips, brows furrowed. "I like …" She bit her red lip. "I like … I like buying knockoff brands instead of designer."

Oh. That wasn't what I'd expected, but knowing that she had designer everything, it was surprising.

She gave me a big grin that didn't reach her eyes, and then she turned onto her back and blew out a deep breath.

"Thank you, Vanessa," I said after a few moments. "I really needed this."

She rested her head against my shoulder and inhaled. "Anytime."

Roman: Pack House. Noon. Lunch with Kylo.

I raised a brow at Roman's text message and sank into my seat at The Night Raider's Café to chat with Raj. It was hard for me to believe that they could be civil and act as if they didn't want to rip each other to pieces. Part of me low-key expected to find Roman sitting on one of the kitchen chairs with a platter holding Kylo's head for lunch.

Vanessa strolled up to our table in a small white tank top and tight black jeans with an iced coffee. "So, should we expect that everyone who has been in contact with Ryker and the rogues might be infected by the darkness or might be influenced by the darkness in some type of way more so than a wolf who hasn't been in contact?" she asked, sitting beside Raj.

"I'm not sure, and I don't think the Moon Goddess even knows." Bouncing my knee up and down, I gazed over at Raj. "But that's a lot of people—every single one of the Lycans, everyone in Roman's pack."

Raj swallowed hard. "Jane."

"How is Jane?" I asked, breaking a coffee-cake muffin into two pieces. "I haven't seen her."

Vanessa frowned. "Neither have I."

"She's been acting off lately. She's been having some nightmares about the rogues capturing me and her and taking us back to their hideout; she wakes up in a cold sweat every morning," Raj said, rubbing a hand across his face. "She told me that she's had bad dreams ever since her parents died though."

Vanessa wrapped her red lips around her straw and sipped. "She never had nightmares before, as far as I knew, not even after her parents died."

"Roman has nightmares sometimes," I admitted. "Sometimes, when he's awake, he stares at nothingness and starts hyperventilating. I've only seen it once, but he's told me that it happens more often than I think."

Raj shook his head. "These nightmares aren't normal. They're fucking terrifying, even for me. Last night, she was screaming at the top of her lungs and then muttering utter nonsense for nearly an hour. When she woke up, she had no recollection of any of it."

Vanessa strummed her fingers against her blue coffee cup. "I want to go see her, but she's always busy."

I opened my phone's Notes app and typed Jane's name. "She could be corrupted."

"Who else?" Vanessa asked.

"Has anyone seen Derek?" I asked.

Since I had gotten back from my weekend away, I hadn't had the chance to check up on him. We had been drifting apart ever since I became leader of the Lycans, and it broke my heart, not having my best friend around.

Vanessa shook her head. "He didn't show up for practice yesterday morning. And ... he's been acting more aggressive, if you ask me. He was all up in my business the other night." She scrunched up her nose and looked at me. "Like, sexually."

I raised my brows. "Did you have sex with him?"

"Oh, no! Gross. He's not even my type and ..." She lowered her voice and looked away. "Ugh, men."

Sighing deeply through my nose, I typed Derek's name and frowned at the thought of my best friend being corrupted by Dolus. "How can we contain this?" I whispered more to myself than to them.

"We need to contact every single pack and ask them about each of their pack members."

"That could take weeks," Vanessa said.

And we didn't have that kind of time.

"It has to be done sooner. We can't allow corruption to spread," I said.

The Lycans were strong, but we alone weren't strong enough against this enemy. We fought rogues, not gods, not corruption this divine. We needed people who couldn't be corrupted so easily, warriors who could possibly withstand these kinds of attacks against the werewolf species and our goddess.

"We need humans," I said. "Ones who are strong and can help us."

"What exactly would a human alliance do for us in this war?" Vanessa asked.

"The Moon Goddess only mentioned werewolves being corrupted, not humans. If we can find some who will help us, we might just have a chance, if the time comes, to get close to Dolus and kill him." I furrowed my brows and sighed, knowing that using humans *might not even work*. "I'm just spitballing ideas here."

Raj stole a piece of my muffin. "I know someone. She knows about the werewolves species and has been training alongside Alpha Ming's pack in the south. If we get her the right training—both physical and mental—she could be as strong as a Lycan."

"Who is she?" I asked.

"Her name is Naomi."

Raj glanced down at his phone as a message from Jane popped up on the screen. "Ming leads practice every morning at ten a.m. If we run there now, we could get there to watch her practice and talk to her."

It would take about an hour to run to his pack and an hour to run back, which would be cutting it close to lunch with Roman and Kylo. But I had more pressing matters on my hands right now than lunch. I needed to gather as many humans and every strong wolf as possible to join the Lycans before corruption spread like wildfire.

Raj's phone rang. "I need to take this to make sure she's all right," he said. "I will meet you there as soon as possible." He slid out of the booth and placed his phone to his ear. "What's wrong, Jane?"

Vanessa nodded to the door. "I'll go with you."

"Are you sure that Roman doesn't need you back at the pack house?"

"No," she said, scrunching her nose. "Derek and I were just going through potential new recruits for this upcoming graduate class, scoping them out and offering some training beforehand to make the pack stronger." She let out a sigh. "But Derek is getting way too flirty. I need a break from him."

After I tossed my muffin in the trash, we shifted into our wolves and ran toward Alpha Ming's pack. My stomach tightened as I thought about the darkness that could be creeping into Derek, seeping into his mind and destroying him slowly.

If Derek were corrupted, it would kill me. Even if we no longer talked every day, even if we talked once a week, he was still my best friend, and I loved him and his family. And I couldn't bear to see him or them hurt. But darkness didn't care about who my best friend was. It sank its claws and slowly became part of someone.

CHAPTER 23

ROMAN

"*Isabella,*" I said through the mind link, tapping my finger against the oak desk.

Kylo sat across from me, scrolling through our old texts and pictures we had taken before Scarlett tore us apart. I didn't think he'd still have those texts. Hell, I deleted all my conversations with him. But Kylo had always been more sentimental than I ever had—because even if he wanted to kill me at one point, we had been friends for so long.

Last night, Kylo and I had talked about Scarlett, Mom, and Isabella until the rain drowned the last of the embers in the bonfire. Though it was awkward as hell, it wasn't as bad as I'd thought it'd be after learning about how he and Isabella had been mates in their past lives. Yet the whole time, I had tried to find something wrong or deceptive about him but come up empty-handed.

Everything he said about his feelings toward Isabella was all completely true.

Isabella hummed on the other side of the mind link. *"Tell Derek to stop being a ho and flirting with Vanessa,"* she said to me. *"I'm at Alpha Ming's pack now. I can't talk. See you soon."*

I gazed at the clock on the wall, just above the window. *"Don't be late for lunch."*

She stayed quiet for a long time. *"I will be,"* she said, mischief in her voice.

My lips curled into a soft smile. I glanced out the window as the wind blew tree branches against it. Rain poured down from the gray sky, beating against the glass in a steady rhythm.

After pushing the list of names of people in my pack who could be corrupted to the middle of the desk, I looked toward Kylo.

"You remember when we used to train together?" Kylo asked, sliding his phone across the desk.

On the screen, there was a picture of us when I was fourteen with my arm slung around his shoulders and a huge grin on each of our faces. Two alphas who didn't know that, one day, an evil girl would tear them apart and a strong luna would reunite them.

"Was this before Scarlett?" I asked.

"You were dating her at the time," Kylo said, snatching the phone back. "I deleted all the pictures of me and her after I rejected her. I couldn't deal with seeing her face in every photo my mother had propped up in her house."

I nodded. "I burned all the pictures with her after finding out Isabella was my mate."

Kylo paused for a long moment and finally sucked in a breath. "Are you still … into that?"

"Into what?" I asked, gaze drifting back to the window.
"Having someone watch?"

He gave the slightest shrug and then glanced back down at his phone as if he regretted even asking. I watched as his face contorted into an array of emotions until, eventually, his expression landed on one of pain—written in the way he furrowed his brows and turned his lips down in a frown.

Rubbing my palm against my jeans, I glanced down at the desk. Isabella's wolf was Kylo's mate, too, and I had already fucked up his chances of a happy life with Scarlett. Even with Isabella being *mine*, how could I refuse him something so precious without feeling like complete shit for a second time?

"I let you watch me throat-fuck her in the hall, didn't I?" I asked him.

Kylo looked up at me with wide eyes. "You knew about me being there?"

"Of course I fucking did. Your voyeuristic ass probably got off on it too," I joked.

Instead of responding, Kylo rubbed the stubble on his cheek. "And Isabella?" he asked.

"You want to watch me fuck her?" I asked, curling my fingers as my jeans tightened at the mere thought of making Kylo watch as I touched Isabella's dripping little cunt. "Lunch. We'll see if she wants it during lunch."

CHAPTER 24

ISABELLA

*R*ain drizzled from the gray-white sky above Alpha Ming's training field. I crossed my arms over my chest and observed the raw and vicious way each warrior fought one another in their human forms, muscle against muscle, strength against strength, grit against grit.

And while everyone fought with such fervor, not one of them looked like just a human.

"Luna Isabella!" Alpha Ming jogged over to me, his chest covered in a layer of rainwater and sweat. He whistled, indicating everyone to take a break, and nodded in my direction. "So, what brings you here?"

"I'm looking for Naomi."

He raised his eyebrows, brown eyes widening. "Why do you need her? Did she do something? She's a nice girl. She—"

"She didn't do anything wrong," I said. "I might need to recruit her for the Lycans, so I need to watch her practice." I stepped closer to him and lowered my voice. "There is a war coming for our kind."

Ming wiped away some beads of sweat with a towel. "With Alpha Kylo? Did he turn the other alphas on you already? It's only been a week since the alphas meeting."

So much had changed since that meeting. At that time, Kylo and I were strangers. Now, we were millennia-old mates. It had been less than seven days, and my wolf felt thousands of years of love for that man.

"No," I said to him. "It is against the God of Corruption, who is hurting the werewolf species. We need to stop him, and that requires us to gather as many humans—who might not be susceptible to his magic—and recruit them as Lycans."

After a few moments, he nodded and then shouted Naomi's name. A short and petite woman with long, soft brown hair jogged over to us, her cheeks flushed pink from training relentlessly. "Yes, Alpha Ming?"

My eyes widened slightly. How could someone her size compete against werewolves who were twice her size and had at least double her strength? She must be good—really damn good—to have even caught Raj's attention.

Ming placed a hand on my shoulder. "This is Isabella, luna of the Silverclaw Pack and leader of the Lycans. She has come to assess you during training. She might need you and your abilities for a mission."

Staring up at me with big brown eyes, she asked, "Me?"

I smiled. "Yes."

"Okay, um," she started, rubbing the back of her neck. "Yes! Sure. Wait, is everything okay though? I'm only a human. I'm not sure if I'll be good enough to train with the Lycans for a mission."

"There is a war coming," I repeated to her. Raj jogged onto the property and shifted into his human, snatching someone's shirt from the side of the field. "We don't have much time. Show me what you've got."

When they all jogged back onto the field, Raj rocked back and forth on his heels next to Vanessa. We watched Naomi stand back up every time after someone pushed her down, outsmart someone before they could outsmart her, drive them into the ground and hold them there before someone had the chance to even touch her.

Though small, she had extraordinary strength, wits, and smarts.

To me, something about her screamed *Lycan*.

Alpha Ming crossed his arms over his chest. "What do you think?"

"She's been training with your pack for a year?" Raj asked, hands on hips.

Ming nodded. "She is quickly becoming one of the strongest and smartest people I have ever trained," he said proudly.

Naomi picked one of the men right off of the ground, held him on her shoulders in a fireman's carry, and slammed him on the dirt, pinning him. He squirmed under her, trying to break free, but she held her position with such force.

"Where'd you find her?" Vanessa asked. "And how did she know about werewolves?"

"She used to go to school with my sister, and Naomi stumbled upon her shifting one day."

"Does she have a mate?" I asked. Maybe she was a luna or was bound to someone who was strong. Though there weren't many werewolves mated with humans nowadays, the Moon Goddess chose a select few strong-willed humans for werewolves.

Ming shook his head. "Not that I know of."

After looking over at Raj, I nodded as the rain continued drizzling around us. "We need her," I said, glancing at Ming.

"And any other humans that you might know of who has her kind of strength."

"I'll ask some other packs to see if there is anyone else, but I'm not sure there is. Not many humans know about werewolves, and if they do, they probably aren't too fond of us," Ming said.

Once we finished talking with Ming, I walked over to Naomi, who was wiping the sweat off her forehead with a towel. "Naomi, if you're willing, I want to ask you to become a Lycan." Her eyes widened, and I continued, "But you need to start training as soon as you can. Tomorrow, if possible."

She looked over to her supportive packmates. "I-I don't know what to say."

Raj rocked back on his heels. "Say yes," he whispered.

"Of course! I would love to!" She grinned and turned in the opposite direction. "Oh gosh … I need to pack."

"Pack whatever you need. Raj"—I gestured to Raj—"will assist you."

After warning the rest of Ming's warriors to prepare for the war, I frowned and walked through the woods toward home. Though all of Ming's warriors were strong and resilient, some of them could've been infected. I gnawed on the inside of my lip.

We didn't know anything about this corruption. How could we know who really had it? I could've already had it and not known about it. Vanessa could be corrupted. And Roman …

How much longer until it spread into our pack? In five days? Two weeks? Maybe three weeks *ago*? It wasn't just a matter of *who*, but a matter of when, how the corruption spread, and how to even diagnose it.

CHAPTER 25

ISABELLA

*I*f lunch with Roman and Kylo was as bad as I thought it was going to be, I would be screwed. After I'd left them last night and after everything that had happened between them, I couldn't even imagine them being civil with each other.

"Roman?" I called as I walked up the stairs, looking for them. "Kylo?"

No answer.

I walked up to the bedroom—the only place in this entire house I hadn't checked yet—and found a note in the center of the bed and a silky black dress underneath it. Scribbled in Roman's messy handwriting, the note read: *Meet us at The Cave for lunch. Don't be later than 12:30 p.m., or there will be consequences.*

Consequences.

Roman's consequences were the *worst*. If they involved Kylo, too ... Goddess, they'd be *terrible*. After fanning myself,

I desperately tried not to get too excited because Roman would never do that—even with that voyeuristic kink. If he knew that Kylo had watched me suck him off at the Lycans' pack house, he'd flip out just because it was Kylo.

Once I showered, I slipped into the dress and sprinted to the car. When I made it to the restaurant, I hopped out of the car and smoothed out my dress. My stomach tightened at the thought of enduring the next hour or so as Roman and Kylo scowled at each other.

The Cave was a suit-and-tie restaurant located right outside the pier. Boats swayed near the docks as people walked on and off them, staring out on the lake. I walked into the building, glancing around at the gloss-finished wooden tables surrounded by men and women dressed in their finest casual attire.

A chandelier hung in the center of the room, hundreds of glass pieces decorating it and propelling bright white light in all directions. I strolled down the aisles and found Roman and Kylo sitting at a table near the back of the restaurant with a half-full bottle of wine between them.

Smiling. Laughing. Talking like they'd never stopped being best friends. I stared at them with wide eyes and wondered just what had happened last night after I left for Vanessa's. This was not how I'd left them.

Roman lifted his nose to the air, inhaled softly, and turned in my direction. When he saw me, his smile turned into a tight-jawed frown. He tapped the watch on his wrist and mouthed the word, *Consequences*, to me.

I gathered all the courage that I had and walked right toward them.

It was going to go great today. Nothing was going to happen. It was not going to be a complete and utter disaster to have lunch with both of these possessive, dominant alphas.

Roman pulled out the chair next to him, gaze raking down

my body, and let out a low, sensual growl. I sat next to him, kissed him on the cheek, and placed my hand on his thigh to calm him down. Or maybe it was to calm myself down.

Grabbing my jaw softly, he said, "I told you to be here at twelve thirty. You're late."

That overwhelming sense of dominance and of old Roman was back, and it was stronger than ever.

I tore my gaze from him, feeling that innate defiance bubbling inside of me, and gazed down at my menu. "Well, I'm here now."

All I could think about was defying him until he forced me to submit to him.

"You kept me and Kylo waiting," Roman continued.

For the first time today, I locked eyes with Kylo. Dark, sinful mystery lay so strongly in those golden eyes of his that I had to look away.

Without sparing either of them a second glance, I arched a brow and looked back down. "You guys had to wait a whole *five* minutes for me. I'm not going to apologize for it."

This would rile Roman up, and I loved to rile him up.

Roman placed his hand on my inner thigh and growled low, the carnal sound making me wet. I grabbed my water to calm myself down, knowing that I wouldn't be able to get out of this. He wouldn't let me get away with saying something like that to him in front of Kylo.

"Touch yourself," he said through the mind link.

I choked on my water, placed a hand on my chest, and coughed. After pressing my thighs closer together so he couldn't touch me himself, I gazed back down at the menu. I had expected something—maybe a harsh punishment when we got home—but not *that*.

"Now, Isabella." He squeezed my knee harder. *"Or I will."*

I scooted my chair closer to the table, hoping that nobody

could see him touch. "So, um, what did you guys talk about last night?"

Kylo arched a brow at Roman and cracked a smirk. "Nothing you need to know about, princess." He leaned back in his seat, biceps flexing through his thin gray dress shirt. "What'd you end up doing? Spend the night with another lover?"

Roman trailed his fingers up my thigh and brushed them against my panties. The scent of mint and pine drifted through my nostrils as he drew his fingers around in small, tortuous circles. I grasped the table, my fingernails digging into the dark, glossy wood.

"If you want to—" I started.

Roman curled his fingers inside my thin, lacy panties and ripped them right off of me.

"Hmm?" Kylo hummed, sipping on his wine.

My wolf purred at the sight of his muscles strained against his top, at the way his full and plump pink lips curled into a cruel smirk.

"If you want to call Vanessa my—"

Roman rested one forearm on the table and thrust his fingers into me, shoving them as deep as they would go. I clenched around him and gulped, heart racing inside my chest.

Goddess, this wasn't really happening, was it?

"Your what?" Kylo asked again.

Had their plan been all along to take me to a restaurant and let Roman touch me while Kylo watched?

My nipples hardened against my push-up bra.

Roman leaned closer to me, his lips against my ear. "Take it off."

"Take what off?" I whisper-yelled, finally directing my attention toward him. Heat crawled up my neck, making my cheeks burn with both embarrassment and pleasure. "You already ripped my underwear."

"Take off your bra."

I shook my head. "No."

"You know that if you don't do it, I will," Roman threatened.

Kylo chuckled to himself over his glass of wine, eyes a dangerous golden color. I clenched my jaw and fumbled with the clip on the damn bra. *Why the hell was I doing this again?* This lunch was supposed to be about talking out our differences, not getting undressed in the middle of a fancy restaurant.

Once I took the bra off, Roman draped it across the huge bulge in his pants. "Relaxed now?"

"No!" I whisper-yelled at him. "I'm not relaxed! My underwear is ripped. I don't have my bra on anymore. You're giving me that *I'm going to fuck you* look. And I'm—"

"Wet," Kylo interrupted, glancing at Roman. "She's wet, isn't she?"

My cheeks flushed, and I growled, "No, I'm not."

Roman grasped my jaw, his fingers still pumping in and out of me. "You are," he said.

My breasts brushed against the edge of the table, and I whimpered quietly to myself. A wave of heat rushed through my body and warmed my core.

Roman tilted his head to the side. "Why are you wet? This is supposed to be a punishment for you."

He pumped his fingers faster into me, and I pressed my lips together.

"I asked you a question, my dear Isabella."

Just as I was about to answer, a man—my savior—dressed in a white shirt, black pants, and a name tag that read *James* approached our table. "Welcome to The Cave. My name is Jimmy. What can I get for you today?"

"Isabella, why don't you go first?" Kylo said.

I parted my lips and then pressed them back together about twenty times. Roman continued to pump his fingers into me, hitting my G-spot nearly every time. I brushed my nipples against the cool table again as they poked right through my silky black dress.

"What would you like?" Roman asked again, fingers moving faster.

Furrowing my brows together, I grasped the menu tighter. "I'll have … the …" I swallowed hard, unable to focus on any of the lunch choices. Why were we even here again? What were we doing out at a nice restaurant, all together? So we could talk? So we could …

Roman brushed his thumb against my clit, rubbing it in fast, rough circles.

"We're waiting, princess," Kylo said, strumming his fingers against his wineglass.

"The pasta," I blurted, pressing my breasts against the table. I gently tugged on my nipples under it and bit my lip at the intense pleasure shooting through my body. "Whatever kind you have. I don't care."

After taking Roman's and Kylo's orders with ease, the waiter left me alone with the two devilish alphas who were staring me down like they were hungry and I was their next savory meal.

"You're mine, Isabella," Roman said through the mind link. *"Every single part of your body is mine."*

He flicked his fingers back and forth, and I grasped the edges of the table, unable to think about anything other than the pressure building in my core.

I glanced over at Kylo and furrowed my brows. He placed his wineglass down and pushed his hand under the table himself, probably stroking his cock through his pants, the same way he had when he watched me take Roman's cock down my throat during the alphas meeting.

Roman wrapped his arm around my shoulders, drew me closer, and placed a hand over my mouth as I moaned loudly into it. He made me stare right up at him as my pussy pulsed on his fingers over and over until I came.

When I came down from my orgasm and relaxed in his arms, he took his fingers out of me and pressed them to my lips, his arm around my shoulders keeping me still. He pushed his fingers into my mouth, and I sucked them desperately.

"Every bit of you is mine," he said through the mind link.

After nodding my head, I took a deep breath, smoothed out my dress, and sat up straight.

Roman leaned close to me, his lips brushing against my ear and his hand on my thigh again. "Next time you disobey me in front of Kylo, you will be on your knees."

My pussy clenched at the mere thought of disobeying Roman and letting Kylo watch him *really* punish me with his hard and throbbing cock. I sipped my water and cleared my throat, trying to cool my flushed cheeks.

I'd just come in the middle of the restaurant by Roman's fingers and while Kylo watched.

"So"—I glanced between Roman and Kylo—"what happened last night?"

"Like I said, princess, nothing you have to know about."

"But … you're … civil …"

Roman nodded his head. "We are."

I sucked on my bottom lip. "But you usually want to rip each other's throats out."

Waiter Jimmy approached the table, juggling all our meals. "Anything else I can do for you?" he asked, setting down the plates in front of us.

When he took our silence as a *no,* he smiled and walked to another table.

I turned back to the alphas and arched a brow. "Hmm? What happened to wanting to kill each other?"

"We just talked," Kylo said.

"About me?" I asked, unsure of about how I felt about this entire thing. My heart belonged to Roman, but my wolf's soul had belonged to Kylo for thousands of years.

"Always thinking you're the topic of conversation, princess." Kylo shook his head, lips curling into a smirk, and leaned forward. "You know, we did talk about you." He looked over at Roman, plump lips parting. "Do you want to tell her that we talked about how submissive she is in bed?"

Roman didn't say anything, just stared at me with curious eyes, as if he wondered how I would react to Kylo's comment.

"You told him that I was submissive?" I asked, brows furrowed.

"I told him that you were a brat," Roman corrected.

"And I told Roman that you seem like a woman who likes to take control, Isabella." Kylo tilted his head and sipped his wine again. "Not be controlled all the time."

If this were a totally different situation, I would give him my meanest, sassiest remark to see if he would take the bait to punish me … but we were out at lunch with my mate sitting next to me, and I was enjoying this conversation a little too much.

Kylo cut his steak, pierced it with his fork, and asked, "Have you ever been in control?"

My heart pounded. Plagued with confusion, I stared between them and shook my head. What the hell was going on with them? Had they actually talked about me *like that* last night after I left them? And why was Roman giving me those domineering eyes, as if he didn't mind Kylo talking to me this way? Why was his hand trailing back up my thigh and making it hard for me to breathe?

Kylo stared at me with his lovely brown eyes as specs of gold appear within them. He brushed his foot against mine under the table. "Do you want to be in control?" he asked again.

I pressed my knees together. *Damn it, Isabella. Calm your ass down.*

Roman squeezed my thigh and gave me a hard stare, his fingers trailing up the inside of my thigh to my wet pussy yet. He pushed two fingers inside of me and let my pussy clench around them. "Relax," he said to me and then nodded toward Kylo. "Ask her again."

Heat warmed my core as he slid a third finger inside of me.

"Isabella, do you want to be in control?" Kylo asked.

Roman stared down at me, lips curled into a smirk. "Or do you like the thought of being dominated by your two mates?"

He curled his fingers into me ever-so softly, and I lost it. My pussy pulsed over and over on him. Ecstasy shot through my body. Everything slowed down.

I grasped his wrist, my body visibly trembling back and forth, and stuck my face into his shoulder. Wave after wave of delight made my body tingle. I leaned back in the seat, waiting for my orgasm to stop but it didn't for minutes.

The thought of being in bed with my two mates at the same time made me feel like sin itself.

CHAPTER 26

ROMAN

*W*ith my fingers still inside of her, Isabella trembled for two whole minutes. Ecstasy had washed over her face as soon as those words left my mouth. I should've hated even suggesting that, one day, I might feel alpha enough to share Isabella with Kylo, but she had such a strong, raw reaction to it that it left me so fucking hard.

I wanted her to come like that again. I never wanted her to stop feeling this good.

We had been through so much fucking pain together that all I wanted was to make her feel like she owned the entire world and everyone in it. She didn't deserve any more pain, and *I* couldn't be the source of it anymore.

When she grasped my wrist and pulled my fingers out of her, I stuck them into my mouth and happily sucked off her juices, tasting how sweet she was for me. Kylo clenched his jaw, moving his hand under the table and watching my mate feel good.

Groaning to myself, I licked off the rest of her from my fingers. I fucking loved letting him get off on watching me pleasure my mate. The insecure part of me wished that this were wrong, wished that I were furious, that she didn't truly like Kylo. But the Moon Goddess had made us mates because we could be strong together, and I was devoted to Isabella even more now that the world was facing corruption.

And Kylo was committed to her too. They'd shared a bond for over seven thousand years.

Realization washing over her features, she widened her eyes. "Roman, I didn't mean to come from what you said … I … I …" she started, shaking her head.

Through our personal mind link, I listened to all her jumbled thoughts, her worry about how this was wrong, heartbreak because she thought I'd be mad, and sorrow for the way she felt about Kylo.

"It's okay," I said through the mind link.

She stared down at the table, more submissively than I had ever seen her. *"No, it's not."*

"Isabella, look at me." I tilted her head toward me and made her stare up at me with those big, innocent eyes, the ones I had fallen in love many times over. "Whose are you?"

She gnawed on the inside of her cheek and peeked at Kylo, then back at me. "I'm yours."

"If I say that something is okay for me, then it's okay."

While she still looked hesitant, she eventually nodded and grabbed her fork. "Okay," she whispered, sitting in silence for a few more moments, the sexual tension slowly dissipating between us.

"We have to do something about Dolus," Isabella said after five minutes. "I've started recruiting humans for the Lycans." Isabella wiped the sauce off her lips with a napkin and placed it on the table. "I hope you both talked about what you're going to do."

"My pack is preparing," Kylo said. "Ready to aid you in any way that you might need."

"You know you always have our pack ready to follow you," I said.

Isabella gave a curt nod. "Raj told me that Jane was having nightmares and is waking him up by screaming. She doesn't remember the nightmares when she wakes up," she said, sipping her wine.

I pressed my lips together, brows furrowing. "Jane's having nightmares? Why didn't I know about this?"

Jane was the only immediate family I had left, and I needed to protect her. If she was having nightmares—unlike the ones that I had of Mom's death—then she was probably more susceptible to corruption than I'd originally thought.

After telling Derek to keep an eye on Jane through text, I pushed my phone into my pocket and finished up lunch. Isabella kept brushing her foot against mine under the table, her fingers dancing across my inner thighs. She had her knees pressed together, yet all I could smell was my dessert when we got home.

When we exited the restaurant, Isabella wrapped her arms around Kylo and pulled him into a tight hug—her round breasts pressed against his torso, her defiant gaze on me, and her bratty smirk plastered on her face.

"Bye, *babe*," she said to him as a way to taunt me.

Her two toe-curling orgasms at lunch must've not been enough for her. My Isabella wanted me to fuck her hard when we got home, and I was going to give her everything that she wanted.

CHAPTER 27

ISABELLA

*A*fter returning to the pack house, I swayed my hips from side to side and walked up the stairs, letting Roman peek up my dress. At lunch, he had been so unbearably hard through his gray suit pants, his cock pressed against the tight material for me to gawk at.

I bet he couldn't wait to get me alone.

When we reached the top of the stairs, Roman pressed me against the nearest wall. "Are you trying to get on my fucking nerves, Isabella?" he asked, soft lips brushing against the mark on my neck. "I told you that the next time you disrespected me in front of Kylo, you'd be on your knees in front of him."

Arching a brow, I pushed my hips back against his to feel his hardness against my ass. "Well, *Roman*, Kylo isn't here." I placed a hand on this bulge and stroked him slowly. "It's just me and you."

He snaked a hand around the front of my throat and

placed his other against my lower back, pulling and pushing me toward our bedroom. "Is that what you think?" he asked, slamming the door shut and shoving me toward the open window.

As I stumbled toward it, I grabbed the windowsill for support—my moonflowers twinkling next to Luna Raya's keychain. My gaze drifted from the petals to the forest outside, and I clenched. Kylo could be out there somewhere, watching us and everything that was about to happen.

Roman grabbed my wrist, tugged me in front of the full-length mirror in our bedroom, and stood behind me. After pulling the straps off my dress and letting my breasts fall out of it, Roman thrust my clothes off and stared at me through the mirror's reflection with those devilishly gold eyes.

"On your knees."

I felt my lips curl into a smirk. "No."

His jaw twitched. "On your knees *now*, Isabella."

"Make me." I narrowed my eyes at him. "*You won't.*"

Snatching a fistful of my hair, he pulled me toward him. "Oh, I will, Isabella," he taunted as he slapped one of my tits. My breast tingled, turning light pink. He growled in my ear, canines grazing up the column of my neck, "You're going to obey every one of my fucking commands. Do you understand me?"

"No, I don't."

After letting out another vicious and carnal growl, he reached around my torso to pinch both my nipples hard between his fingers. I clenched, heat warming my core, and grasped his wrists, pain shooting through me. I held on for as long as I could, the discomfort becoming almost unbearable but making my pussy so damn wet for him.

"Fine," I said. "I'll obey you."

"It's too late for that. You've already made your choice."

He squeezed my nipples harder and harshly pulled them

toward the ground. I stumbled to my knees, my face right in front of his bulge, and stared up at him. When he finally released his grip on them, I whimpered, grasped my breasts, and rubbed them gently, already feeling sore.

With one hand, Roman pulled his shirt over his head, revealing his carved abdomen. I slowly gazed up his torso, admiring how shredded and cut his body was from years of training, running, and fighting for his pack.

"Take off my pants."

I drew my fingers down the veins that led from his abdomen to his belt buckle and then pulled down his pants, letting his hard cock spring out and nearly hit me right in the face. Grasping it in my hand, I inhaled deeply and shuddered from the smell of two woodsy scents.

Roman grabbed my throat. "I didn't tell you that you could touch it."

"I don't ca—"

He shoved his cock into my mouth and all the way down my throat. "Do you care now, Isabella?" he asked domineeringly.

I opened my mouth wider to respond but only got out a wet and sloppy gag.

"What was that?"

All I wanted was for him to thrust into me, use me in all the ways he wanted, show Kylo who my alpha really was.

After pinching my nipples hard again, he said, "Off your heels."

When I knelt tall for him, my mouth still stuffed full, he released his grip on my nipples and massaged my breasts. "Are you going to be a good girl for me?" he asked.

I let out another wet gag and looked up at my mate's smirking face.

He grasped a fistful of my hair and forced me to look into the mirror. "Look at yourself," he ordered. Spit rolling down my chin, eyes filling with tears, cheeks flushing a deep red, I gagged on him as he brushed two fingers down the huge bulge in my throat. "Look at my cock all the way down your throat."

As I glanced back up at him through teary eyes and my mouth wide open to try to breathe, he forced me to turn back toward the mirror. "Now, touch yourself. Put two fingers into your pussy and fuck it the same way you want me to fuck you."

Slobbering from my mouth, I trailed two fingers against my slit and slid them into my wet hole with ease. My pussy immediately clenched around them, as if it had been waiting to be filled again since lunch. Through the mirror's reflection, I watched as I slowly pumped my fingers in and out until I couldn't handle the sheer amount of pressure anymore. I wildly thrust them into me as my juices dripped onto our bedroom floor.

When I closed my eyes for a brief moment, Roman tightened his grip on my hair. "I told you to watch yourself," he said.

I gazed back into the mirror at how utterly ruined I was.

Roman growled lowly and stared intently down at me, "I want you to see exactly how you looked to Kylo when I shoved my cock down your throat at the alphas meeting."

My eyes widened, yet I didn't stop thrusting my fingers up into me. Instead, I pounded them faster and harder and more desperately. Roman had known Kylo was watching the entire time? He had forcefully pushed me onto my knees in front of him as a display of dominance and inferiority.

"You thought I didn't know?" he asked, tilting his head and sneering down at me. "I pushed you down onto your knees and shoved my cock down your throat"—he pushed himself further down my throat—"not because I wanted him to know that you were mine, but because I wanted you to know."

More spit dripped down my chin, and I found myself willingly bobbing my head back and forth and gagging on him until I could barely breathe. Goddess, this felt so much better than I'd thought it would.

"Anyone can fantasize about shoving themselves into your pretty little mouth"—he groped my breasts—"or between these nice tits"—his gaze drifted between my legs to my glistening pussy—"or into your tight pussy … but only I can do it."

He grabbed my free hand and placed it around my own throat. "Squeeze," he ordered.

I tightened my grip around his dick inside of me—so he could feel just how tight I was for him—and then let him face-fuck me hard with his hands tangled in my hair and his hips smacking against my lips.

As I thrust my fingers up hard into me, my palm hit my clit each time. I stared up into his golden eyes, letting my alpha dominate me. Any way that he wanted, anywhere he wanted, anytime he wanted, I would let him take me.

I was his.

When his thrusting became too much, I dug my claws into his thighs. He pulled out of me almost immediately, tugged me to my feet, ordered me to place my hands on the mirror, and thrust into me from behind.

"Roman!" I screamed as he filled me.

Not bothering to stop or slow down, he curled his fingers into my hips. Brown hair flopping against his forehead, sweat dripping down his muscular chest, canines bared at my reflection, he let out a ferocious growl. My cunt tightened around his cock, and I glanced out the window.

Just outside our bedroom window, Kylo stood as a large brown wolf and watched my mate destroy my sopping tight pussy. Two golden eyes glowed in the darkening forest the same way they must've for the past seven thousand years.

I curled my fingers into the wooden mirror frame. "Harder, Roman."

Roman looked out of the window, lifted one of my legs into the air to showcase the way he rammed his cock into my wet bare cunt to Kylo, and then rubbed my clit hard. I tightened my grip on the mirror.

"Please, come inside of me," I pleaded. "Please, I need it."

"I'm not finished with you yet. I'm going to fuck this pussy until I'm ready to come. You understand that, right, Isabella?" he asked.

I whimpered but nodded.

He grasped a fistful of my hair again. "You respond with, *Yes, Alpha.*"

"Yes, Alpha," I said in a raspy breath. As he continued to fuck me with his fingers moving faster around my clit, I gazed out of the window, unable to handle the pressure anymore. "Don't you want to claim what's yours in front of Kylo?" I asked. "Don't you want to come inside of me and let him watch, so he knows who I belong to?"

Roman groaned in my ear, his entire body shuddering behind me, and slowed his thrusts. "Isabella, you're testing me."

"Let him watch you fill me with all your cum."

"Isabella."

"Do you want me to scream your name when you do it?"

He grasped my hips, thrusting hard and deep one last time inside of me. I grasped on to the mirror, watched him part his lips almost instinctively as he came, and moaned as wave after wave of pleasure washed through me.

Our raspy and ragged breaths filled the air. Roman pulled out of me, picked me up, and laid me on his chest on the bed. I rested my head right over Roman's heart and drew patterns on his abdomen, trying to calm my racing heart.

"Are you okay?" Roman asked after a few quiet moments, gently rubbing my throat. "I didn't hurt you, did I?"

My lips curled into a smile. "No," I said softly. "You didn't hurt me."

Slinging an arm around my shoulders, he pulled me up to him and kissed my nose. "Why are you quiet then? You always have something coming out of this bratty mouth of yours."

I brushed a strand of hair off his forehead, my stomach tightening. "You're comfortable with Kylo watching?" I asked. Sure, I knew he had a thing for people watching us have sex, but I hadn't thought he'd ever want Kylo to join in on the fun.

"You don't like it?" he asked, pulling away slightly to look at me. "I thought you would."

"Oh no, I loved it! I just … it's Kylo," I said, whispering the last few words.

After blowing out a hesitant breath, Roman gave me half a smile. "You know that Kylo and I have done that before, when we were younger. We talked last night about Scarlett, my mom, and you …"

"You never told me that Kylo's dad did that to your mom …"

He ran a hand across his face, sat up, and leaned against the headboard, staring out into the now-desolate forest. "He did, and I blamed Kylo for it, ripped away his mate, and made him feel like shit. I shouldn't have done it, but I didn't have anyone by my side at the time. Jane was always with Vanessa, and I had to man up and lead this pack before the rogues killed us all. I was stupid and broke a bond that couldn't ever be replaced. I never apologized or even talked to him until yesterday.

"Listen, I'm not going to lie and say that I'm on board with this entire thing between you and him—because I'm not yet. But I took away his chances with his first mate, and you and your wolf mean so much to me. I want you both to be happy."

I pressed my lips together, feeling the warmth spread through my body.

Moonlight flooded in through the window and bounced off Roman's golden eyes. "But," he started, grasping my chin, "if you *ever* moan Kylo's name when *you're with me*, like you did with Cayden, I will lock you in this bedroom, fuck you until you're carrying my pups, and kill him."

While I knew Roman was deathly serious, all I could think about was, "Pups?"

"Pups," he repeated softer this time. The word sounded so satisfying, coming out of his mouth. He interlocked our fingers and pulled our hands against his chest. "I want pups. Do you?"

Pups! My wolf purred. *Mate wants pups!*

It was the first time since meeting Kylo that my wolf had decided to speak up about Roman.

We want pups!

"Do I want pups?" I asked myself.

These past few weeks, I had been too caught up in the Lycans' business to even think about our future. And that was a mistake because with this war coming, I didn't know how much longer we had together. Nothing was certain in this world.

Butterflies erupted inside my stomach. I jumped into his arms. "I want a bunch of them."

I could only imagine Roman running around the property, chasing the kids through the forest, tossing them over his shoulder, and glancing at me when they fell asleep in his arms.

But where would Kylo fit in? How would he fit in? Would he even fit into my future at all?

Roman held me tight to him. "I promise to always protect you and our pups. Whatever trouble comes our way, Isabella"—he lifted my chin just enough so I could stare up into his eyes—"I will protect you with my life."

Burying my head into his chest, I held on to him for dear life because maybe it wasn't me who needed the protection from the corruption barreling our way; maybe it was he who needed it.

CHAPTER 28

ISABELLA

$\mathcal{R}$oman tensed and instantly sat up in our bed, ripping the gray blankets off us. "Fuck, I wanted to check on Jane today." He tugged on a green henley shirt, which brought out those piercing hazel eyes.

I sat up with my mind in a daze and tugged my dress over my head. "I can mind-link Raj if you want me to," I said, brushing out the knots in my hair with my fingers.

Moonlight drifted in through the window, glowing against the moonflower petals. I swept my fingers against the soft edges and stared out into the eerie forest. While some wolves howled and ran through the woods, it all seemed a bit too calm out there.

"It's late," I said to him. "She and Raj are probably asleep."

"I still need to make sure she's okay. I check on her every day."

"I thought you said at lunch that you assigned Derek to oversee her, after learning about Dolus?" I asked, following

155

him to the door. "Wouldn't he mind-link you if she wasn't okay?" When he walked out of the room, I followed him. "Never mind. Let's just go."

Turning around, he grabbed my hand and paused. Instead of telling me to stay here and that he had this under control, like he had so many times before, he smiled. "Thank you."

My chest tightened, butterflies buzzing around in my stomach. Whatever had happened these past few days when I was gone *and* when Roman and Kylo talked must've really changed Roman. Instead of getting angry and telling me what to do, Roman was actually communicating with me now.

I wasn't just a liability to him anymore. I was his luna.

After shifting into our wolves, we ran to Jane's house to find all the upstairs lights on and Raj's car not out front, like it usually was at this time. Maybe Raj was still getting Naomi settled in at the Lycans' … but I had left him to do that hours ago. He should've been home by now.

Roman lifted his nose to the air and sniffed. "Derek isn't here. I told him to watch her whenever Raj wasn't here." He knocked on the front door with the side of his fist.

Nobody answered.

When he knocked on it again, Jane ripped open an upstairs window. "What the hell?"

We stepped away from the door and glanced up at the window.

"Open the door, Jane," Roman said.

She pulled her silky maroon robe tighter around her body. "What do you want? It's almost midnight, and I was about to fall asleep."

"I need to see you," Roman said.

"And where's Raj?" I added.

Once she rolled her eyes, she slammed the window and appeared at the front door a few moments later. I followed

Roman into the house, glancing around at anything that seemed out of place. Raj didn't just disappear, and Derek always followed orders.

"Did Derek come by?" Roman asked Jane, eyes scanning the room and lingering on the stairs. He knew that Derek wasn't here. It was almost obvious by the way this house reeked of perfume and only Jane's scent.

Jane pointed to the stairs. I hurried past her, my heart racing at the thought of Derek possibly being gone, and pushed open every door on their second floor to find any sign of him. Yet there was nothing, except a bag of Derek's clothes and a couple of his journals scattered over the bed, as if they had been searched through.

Typical Derek move to make a mess of things, but … something still didn't seem right.

Derek *always* followed orders. He wouldn't just leave without telling Roman *or* Jane.

"Derek," I said through the mind link. Yet I received no response.

Uneasiness built in the pit of my stomach. Derek couldn't be gone. He was just out. He had to be out. Maybe on a run in the forest or back at his home, getting some underwear or something else that he had forgotten.

When I rushed back down the stairs, Jane scowled at Roman with her arms crossed over her chest. "Can you not butt into my life?" She seethed at him. "I'm not having any nightmares. You don't have to worry about me. That's my mate's job."

Before Roman could say something snarky back to her, I placed my hand on his forearm, curling my fingers around it. "Where's Derek?" I asked her, only thinking the worst. What if Dolus had taken him or corrupted him already? Vanessa had said he was acting weird.

"He's upstairs," Jane said, hiking back her thumb toward

the stairs. "I told him I was going to bed half an hour ago. He said that he wasn't going anywhere because someone"—she glared at Roman—"told him that I needed to be watched."

Claws digging into Roman's skin, I shook my head to keep myself from growling viciously at her. "Well, he's not here," I said through clenched teeth.

Derek was my best fucking friend, and Jane seemed like she couldn't give two fucks about him missing from her own house.

Roman gently rubbed my shoulder. *"Calm down. We'll find him."*

But I couldn't just calm down. He wouldn't have left. Something wasn't right.

"He did seem a bit"—Jane tapped her index finger against her lips—"weird."

"Isabella," Raj suddenly said through the mind link.

"Where are you?" I asked, annoyed, through the link. *"I—"*

"We have a problem."

I stormed away from Jane and Roman, walking out of the house and shutting the door rather harshly behind me. *"What the hell do you mean? Derek is gone, and Jane has been here alone. Where are you?"*

Cranberry bushes rustled on the side of the house. I lengthened my claws, readying to attack whoever was hiding in them. A raccoon popped his head out of the bush and scurried into the forest with three cranberries in his small hands.

"Derek was gone when I got home," Raj said through the link, breathing hard, as if he was sprinting. *"I went out to find him while Jane slept. I picked up his scent leading off Roman's property. And ..."* He paused. *"Hold on."*

The mind link went silent, and I prayed to the Moon Goddess that wherever Derek had gone off to, he was safe.

But deep down, I knew that he wasn't. A sane Derek wouldn't have left the property without telling anyone.

"Meet me at the pack house, Raj," I said through the mind link. Tears brimmed in my eyes.

Plagued with fear and anxiety, I ran back to the pack house without telling Roman.

And when I made it to his office, I collapsed in his seat and thrust my hands into my hair. *"Roman, stay with Jane. I ran back to the pack house. Meet me here in an hour with any information that you can get out of Jane about Derek's disappearance."*

As I turned on my phone to text Derek, Raj rushed into the room and closed the door. Pushing a hand through his thick black hair, Raj paced back and forth. "It doesn't make sense. I settled Naomi into the Lycans' and came home to see Jane in the living room. She told me that Derek had gone to sleep, but … something was wrong. I could just feel it. I brought Jane to bed, wanting her to try to get a good night's sleep tonight, and went to check on Derek." He paused for a long moment. "He wasn't there."

My stomach turned. "Why didn't you tell me this when you found out?"

Raj rubbed a hand over his face. "I thought that he went out to shift or to run, so I went to look for him."

"And?"

"And his scent led me to the borders. I talked to some patrol guards, who told me they saw him leave with a woman." He blew out a breath through his nose. "None of them saw the woman's face."

After shaking my head, I walked to the window and stared out into the never-ending forest. "You know that Derek wouldn't just leave and go against Roman's orders. Roman would have his ass if anything happened to Jane."

159

Unless Derek had found his mate at Jane's house, this had to be the workings of Dolus.

Suddenly, the office door swung open.

Vanessa rushed in and threw her arms around me. "Goddess, I'm so glad you're safe." She pulled me tight to her chest, rubbing my back. "I'm sorry. Roman told me what happened."

Overcome with anxiety, I took a deep breath, inhaling her scent, and relaxed slightly. "It's okay, Vanessa."

"Are you okay?" she asked.

"I'm fine," I lied.

Who the hell was the woman that Derek had been with? Why couldn't anyone see her face? Where had she taken him? She didn't have a recognizable scent, so she couldn't be in this pack or even anyone that Raj had met before.

So many scenarios played over through my mind.

Raj leaned against Roman's desk, staring at the floor, as if he was deep in thought. "What do you want to do?" he asked.

I squeezed Vanessa's hands harder. If this were Dolus, our Goddess must've been in trouble, and this was the beginning of a long, arduous war. I hadn't thought that he would be here so soon. I'd thought that we'd have some time even if it was just a few more days.

"We prepare for war," I said, straightening my back, drawing my hands from Vanessa's, and crossing my arms. "I want five of our best trackers out there, searching for any trace of Derek and this woman."

"We have trackers," Vanessa said.

"I only want trackers from the Lycans. Everything that happens from here on out needs to be overseen by us. I know how each of the warriors on my team acts. If something is off with them, I will know. I can't keep track of the corrupted warriors I don't know."

And if something happened, it would be my fault.

CHAPTER 29

ROMAN

*D*erek was Isabella's best friend, was one of my best warriors, and was gone because of me. After learning about Dolus and about Jane having nightmares that she couldn't remember, I'd assigned him to watch Jane at all times. I hadn't thought that this would happen.

Thirty minutes ago, Raj had told me he'd watch Jane until morning, so I could work, but all I could seem to do now was pace around my office in panic as Isabella and Kylo talked tensely outside. I ran a callous hand over my face and shook my head.

Fuck. Fuck. Fuck. Fuck. Fuck. Fuck. Fuck.

This shouldn't be happening. Not in my pack. Not so soon.

The last time I had seen Derek, he'd seemed perfectly fine. Nothing had seemed off about him.

When my phone buzzed in my pocket, I pulled it out without checking the number and held it to my ear. "Did you find anything?" I asked, hoping to the Moon Goddess that Cayden had found something.

For a few moments, the line was silent, except the steady and soft sound of breathing.

"Roman," Scarlett purred on the other end. "Roman, do you miss me?"

My breathing hitched, and I tensed. "Scarlett, what did you do?"

She giggled. "I didn't do anything."

"I'm not playing games with you."

"You should, Roman. I know how much you always liked playing games with me," she said.

Memories of us that I desperately tried to suppress flooded through my mind. I didn't try to forget them because I still thought and cared about her like that, but because I hated myself for ever getting involved with her in the first place.

I hated that I hadn't waited for Isabella for my first time to be special.

I hated how Scarlett had taken advantage of me while I was hurting.

I hated that I had driven a barrier between Kylo and his mate.

"Whatever you're doing," I said, "needs to stop. Where is Derek?"

"Don't you ever think about all the games we played together? All the late nights of sneaking out and fucking in Kylo's own bed?" she asked, mischief in her voice. She was holding something back and was waiting for the perfect moment to say it; I could hear it in that screechy little voice of hers.

I growled.

Scarlett giggled through the phone. "I heard that Kylo's sneaking around with your mate now, just like we used to.

How does it feel, knowing that your Isabella wants to fuck your ex–best friend?"

Outside my window, Kylo was gently rubbing Isabella's back as she ran a hand through her long brown hair. Brows drawn together, she stared at him with so much hurt, heartbreak, and even love in her eyes.

"Their relationship is none of your concern, Scarlett."

"You don't like it, do you?"

While Scarlett was trying hard to break me, I wouldn't let it happen. I'd *never* let it happen again. I loved Isabella and didn't want to see her hurt if she found Derek dead. I'd do anything to get him back for her and protect her from the wrath of Scarlett.

Scarlett answered herself with a laugh. "I didn't think you would. That's why I called actually. I wanted to give you a chance to prove yourself to her, a chance to find Derek and become Isabella's hero again, so she gets her filthy hands off of my Kylo."

I slammed my fist into the wall, creating a hole the size of my hand in the drywall beside my bookcase. "Kylo isn't yours anymore, Scarlett," I said through my teeth.

If Scarlett thought that she could come right back as if nothing had ever happened between us and tear Kylo from Isabella this time and make *my* Isabella hurt, she had another thing fucking coming.

And besides, nothing came that easily with Scarlett. I bet she wanted me to get angry over Kylo, so she could break me and control me too. But if that's what it took to get Derek back for Isabella, then that was how I'd act.

After blowing out a loud breath, I growled, "But I fucking hate that son-of-a-bitch."

Scarlett gave another throaty laugh. "I thought you might say that. Meet me in Galsop tonight, and I'll give you any information that I have about Derek."

Galsop was hours away.

"I won't make it by sunrise," I said. *And I'd have to leave Isabella alone ...*

"Better run quick," Scarlett said, and then she hung up the phone.

With rage running through my veins, I hurled my phone at the wall. She wanted to play this sick sort of game, like she had years ago, and I would play right back. This time, I wouldn't be a fool.

Throwing the pack house door open, I grabbed Isabella's hand and gestured for Kylo to follow us into the pack house, so nobody could hear us. For Derek to have been taken so easily, there had to be a mole in this pack. Someone must've been helping Scarlett.

"What's wrong?" Isabella asked, staring up at me with big, fear-filled eyes. "Did you find Derek? Is he ... is he dead?"

I grasped her hands and placed my lips on her knuckles. "I have to meet Scarlett."

She pulled her hands away from mine and glanced at my phone lying in pieces on the ground. "You were talking to Scarlett?" she whispered, voice breaking.

"Scarlett?" Kylo asked, staring at me with that *are you seriously considering this* look.

"She called me with information about Derek. She's playing games," I said, hoping that she'd trust me to handle this myself. Isabella was strong and smart, but Scarlett was corruption at its finest. She always had been. "If I meet her, I can get any information that she has about Derek."

Isabella tugged me close by the wrist. "I'm going with you. I'm not letting her ... not letting her corrupt you." She shook her head and looked at the scuffed wooden floor between us. "I can't lose you."

Cupping her face in my hands, I made her look up at me. "I love you, Isabella. And you know that I know you're strong and you can fight and you can protect even me, but I have to go alone. If you go, she'll try to kill you, and she really won't give me any information about Derek. We'll be back at square one."

"No," she said, shaking her head. "I'm not letting you go."

"Listen to me, Isabella. I don't know how long I'll be gone. You have to stay here. You have the Lycans to take care of and a war to prepare for. If you come with me and Dolus makes an appearance here, you'll regret it." I brushed my knuckles against her cheek. "Trust me to handle this, like I've grown to trust you."

She swallowed hard, tears filling her eyes. "I don't want to lose you," she said softly.

I kissed her lips and rested my forehead against hers. "You're not going to lose me. I'll be back home as soon as I can. But"—I glanced over at Kylo, who stood with his arms crossed by the door—"while I'm gone, you will stay with Kylo."

Kylo stood up straighter, eyes widening.

Isabella tensed and stared up at me. "Kylo?" she asked. Without even breaking eye contact with me, she said, "Kylo, I need to talk to Roman alone."

Without another word, Kylo walked out of the pack house and closed the door behind him. Before she could even argue with me, I held a finger to her lips and smiled when she pressed them together. She loved to defy me, and I loved when she did it … but something about her submitting when I needed her got me every time.

"Yes, I want you to stay with Kylo," I said. "Just this once."

"But—"

"I trust you, Isabella. I know that your wolf wants to be with him. I'll never be completely comfortable with our situation," I admitted. "But I know that for you and your wolf to be strong, you need to be with him as much as you need to be with me."

From the way her brows furrowed to the way she gulped, she had hesitation written all over her face. "Roman, my wolf can't control herself around him," she whispered, breaking eye contact with me to stare out the window at him. "I've been trying to control her for so long, but she just keeps retaliating against me more and more. What if …"

"I have one rule and one rule only when you stay with him," I said, taking a deep breath and not even wanting to think about this happening—especially not when I was gone. "No sex." I seized her jaw and forced her to look up at me. "No sex, Isabella," I repeated more for myself than for her. "He doesn't put his cock inside of you." I grasped her ass in my hand. "Not here." I brushed my fingers against her pussy through her pants. "Not here." I trailed them up the center of her body to her lips and stuck one of my fingers in her mouth. "And certainly not here."

She stared up at me with those big blue eyes and closed her lips around my finger. Goddess, if it were a better time, I'd take her right here.

Instead, I pulled my finger out of her mouth and asked, "Do I make myself clear?"

After a few silent moments, she nodded her head. "I promise, Roman."

CHAPTER 30

ISABELLA

*N*either Kylo nor I said a word to each other on our run to his pack house. My mind buzzed with thoughts about how to lead the Lycans to victory; if Roman would come home, corrupted because of Scarlett; and when I could leap onto Kylo and—

No, I said to my wolf, scolding her for making me think such sinful things about Kylo. It was the first night when I'd be with him *with* Roman's permission, but that didn't mean she was going to control me the entire night. *We're not doing that with Kylo.*

Pleeeease?

No. We're going to stay at his house until Roman gets back, and that's it.

After she hummed at me and said, *That's what you think,* she disappeared into the back of my mind. I followed Kylo through the woods, his pine scent keeping me relatively calm despite my worst fears coming true.

I had wanted to put up more of a fight with Roman, but he was right. Roman trusted me with Kylo and finally had put his faith in my abilities. The least I could do was trust him back. Nothing would happen between him and Scarlett. He would do what he had to do and kill her after he found Derek.

Before I had left Roman's property, I had given orders to some Lycans to guard every pack in the area, to interrogate any suspicious wolves, and to oversee tests given to wolves suspected of being corrupted.

When we approached the gorge, Kylo stopped and nudged his snout against mine. We didn't have a mind link connection yet, but I knew he wanted me to jump across it. I walked to the edge of the cliff, gazed over at the other side, and swallowed hard.

It was a long jump. I'd need a running start. And even then, I didn't know if I'd make it.

Kylo nudged me again, walked back a few feet, and sprang across it, landing on the other side with a thud. I gnawed on the inside of my lip and followed his movements, just barely making it to the other side too. Stumbling to keep my balance, I knocked some rocks off the cliff and listened to them fall hundreds of feet, striking against the shallow lake below us.

After smacking his paw against my hind leg to get me away from the edge, Kylo led me through parts of the forest I hadn't ever been to before tonight. We ran for five minutes and approached warriors who stood stoically at his borders in the foggy forest.

Yellow light blazed through the many front windows of Kylo's large red-oak cabin. We walked up the stone and shifted into our humans. Kylo grabbed a spare change of clothes near the front entrance and ushered me inside.

Though the pack house was much grander and more spacious than ours, it had such a lonely feel to it.

I looked around the living room and drew my fingers against the brown leather couch. "Do you live here alone?"

"Kylo!" a woman shouted from one of the other rooms. "Is that you? Is everything okay?"

I stared down the hallway, my heart pounding inside my chest. Kylo had a woman living with him? Maybe she was just his sister or a cousin or …

My wolf growled lowly, and I pressed my lips together to shut myself up.

"Yes?" he responded, staring at me with those devilishly dark eyes.

An older woman with graying blonde hair, wrinkles near her eyes, and a grin that matched Kylo's stepped out of the room, staring down at a photo album. She walked all the way down the hall toward us, without even noticing me. And when she looked up from her book, she widened her eyes.

"Oh, I didn't know you had a guest," she said, smiling sweetly at me.

Warmth spread through my chest. She reminded me a bit of Luna Raya.

"This is Isabella," Kylo said, resting his fingers on my upper back.

"Isabella," she repeated, turning toward me. She glanced back at him and raised her brows. "I thought Alpha Roman was her mate?" Suddenly, she furrowed her brows at him in anger. "What'd you do to him? What did—"

"He didn't do anything," I assured. When Kylo's mom turned to me, I gulped. "I … we …"

"It's complicated, Mom."

Complicated. That was exactly how I would describe our relationship too. How else could I explain my attraction and connection to Kylo? It was anything but normal to be one of the two original divine wolves.

After pausing and nodding, she glanced back down at the photo album and smiled at us. "Oh, well … this can wait another night, Kylo. We can finish making it tomorrow. I'll leave you two alone."

I smiled at the mere thought of Kylo—the big, bad alpha—making a cute photo album with his mother. Grasping her forearm, I shook my head. "I don't want to intrude. Don't change your plans because of me. I'm just staying the night in one of Kylo's spare rooms; that's all."

"Nonsense. This boy has been talking about you nonstop." She held the book to her chest as Kylo's cheeks turned the faintest color of red at the mention of talking about me. "I'm not going to barge in on the only night that you two can spend together."

Before Kylo could usher his mother out the front door, she turned around and pointed a finger at his chest. "Don't you go hurting her," she said to him. "And don't for a second act like your father did with Luna Raya."

Kylo lowered his voice. "You know that I wouldn't do that, Mom."

She kissed his cheek and patted him on the back. "Good." She looked back at me. "It was nice meeting you, dear."

After she shut the door behind her, Kylo turned back to me.

I lingered by the couch, nervously running my finger in circles against the leather. "Your mother didn't have to leave."

"Afraid of spending time with me alone, princess?" Kylo leaned against the wall with one foot propped up on it, his huge arms crossed over his chest, and those breathtaking gold eyes. He and I both knew the answer to the question was a big, fat yes.

I tore my gaze away from the way his muscles flexed with ease under his shirt. "No," I lied.

Roman had told me no sex, and I had to get my damn wolf under control because she just wanted to rip his clothes off right here, right now.

My breath caught in the back of my throat when he stepped closer to me.

He brushed his fingers up my forearm and trapped me between him and the couch, his knee between my legs. "You should be."

I gulped and stared into his eyes, trying not to let him get to me, yet my stomach tingled with butterflies.

My wolf whispered, *Kiss him,* to me.

I glanced down at his plump lips, wondering how soft they'd feel against mine.

Would they even be soft? Or would they be rough?

Pressing passionately against mine. Devouring all my little moans. Giving me exactly what I had craved since the Moon Goddess told us our wolves were mates who had lived seven thousand years together.

"Where am I sleeping?" I asked, my mouth parched.

After staring down at me for a few long moments, he grabbed my hand and pulled me to the room at the end of the hallway. With gray brick walls, black decor, and a California king–size bed in the center, this didn't look like a spare at all.

"Get changed into any of my clothes, if you don't want to wear this." He gestured down to the oversize shirt I'd put on after we shifted. "We're going out."

When I raised my brow, he locked his fingers around mine. Sparks shot through me like electricity; this feeling was only usual with Roman. I went to pull my hand away, but he held it tighter.

"You've worked all day, and we don't ever get time alone. Let me take you out, princess."

After staring up into his captivating eyes, I tore my gaze away and nodded. Maybe if I went out with him, my wolf would be satisfied. And plus, a nice dinner or even a drink at the bar was needed. I didn't know when I'd get another stressless night like this with this war.

I closed his bedroom door and found a pair of jeans that I had to roll up about three times so they'd fit me, a belt so the pants wouldn't fall down, and a tight white V-neck in his closet. Before stepping out of the room, I glanced around it and realized just how boring and plain his life must be without a mate.

Roman's and my room was decorated with pictures and moonflowers, items from our little adventures. But Kylo only had a picture of him and his mother in a frame on the night-stand and bare brick walls. There wasn't even a pair of slutty pink panties that some chick might've left here or condoms in one of the nightstands or anything that told me he had people over on the regular.

I wonder when was the last time he had sex, my wolf said to me, mid-search.

I huffed at her and walked to the door. This was what I got for snooping.

Kylo stood in the living room in a fresh pair of ripped jeans and a shirt that clung to every one of his muscles. He held out his hand for me, and I wrapped my arm around it, hoping that he'd keep his hands to himself tonight because I didn't know if I'd be able to.

Yet after two drinks and a night of innocent flirting, I found myself lying in his bed with him and counting the stars through his wide bedroom window to keep myself from begging him to touch me. My whole body felt warm, scorching almost, next to his.

All night at the bar, my wolf had been giddy, incessantly telling me to kiss him, preparing me for this moment. Part of me wished that he'd grab my face already and kiss me, so this feeling inside of me would just go away.

Kylo brushed a strand of hair from my face, fingers caressing against my skin so softly that it gave me butterflies.

I glanced over at him and found myself turning toward him. "If the Moon Goddess could grant you one wish, what would it be?"

Pausing for a long moment, he glanced at the space between us. "There are a lot of things I'd wish for," he said.

"Well, you only have one." I poked him in the hard abdomen. "Make it good."

He rested his hand around my waist and pulled me closer to him. "If I had one wish at this very moment, I'd …" He looked down at my lips and then back into my eyes. "I'd wish that I had killed my father before he hurt Roman's mother."

My eyes widened, and I curled into his chest. I didn't know what about his answer got me, but it did. "Really?" I whispered.

"Really," he said with so much pure honesty. "What he did hurt everyone so much. My mother. Your pack. My and Roman's friendship. If I could take it back, I'd do it in a heartbeat. I think about it every night."

I stared at the man that I realized I knew so little about and smiled. Something about him made me want to stay up until all hours of the night, learning about him. This connection between us just grew stronger and stronger.

He curled his arm tighter around me and pulled me a few inches closer until our lips were centimeters from each other's. "What would you wish for? And be selfish with your wish," he said, minty breath fanning my lips. "Tell me what you want right now. What's the one thought running through your mind?"

I gulped nervously, unable to open my mouth to say anything because I didn't trust myself not to press my lips to his right then and there. My wolf purred at our closeness. The only word that I wanted to scream out was, *You.*

But I couldn't get myself to say it.

Not yet. Not when Roman wasn't here.

So, I tucked my head into Kylo's chest and pulled myself closer to him. By the way that he wrapped his arms around me, I could tell that he didn't need my answer to know exactly what it was.

CHAPTER 31

ROMAN

*I*t took all night to run to the desolate lands that
Scarlett had called Galsop Village. The stores were
boarded up with thick silver, so rabid wolves couldn't break
in and destroy everything. Car doors had been left wide open
with their keys still in the ignitions. Graffiti littered almost
every wall in sight. And while Scarlett's pack resided only a
few miles from here, I couldn't find anyone anywhere.

Cayden and Kylo had mentioned that this part of the
forest was at war with each other, but this looked far worse.
With land scarce around these parts, entire packs of wolves
wouldn't just abandon a perfectly livable village because of
conflict.

I sucked in a deep breath, kept my claws drawn in case
someone attacked, and walked farther into the village, scanning the area. Scarlett had to be here somewhere. By the
looks and scent of the place, she had come here alone.

Walking into the pub—the only place that hadn't been

boarded up—I inhaled the thick, repulsive scent of blood coming from the stairs. It flowed from the first stair and created a pool of fresh blood at the bottom.

Someone's here, my wolf said in my mind.

Instead of just looking for Scarlett like I should've been doing, I walked up the creaking stairs, doubled over when I reached the top, and puked into the flow of blood. Bodies were littered around the room, eyes dug out of their sockets, slashes in every one of their necks, limbs hanging from the ceiling fan.

"Fuck," I whispered to myself, spitting out the rest of the vomit.

Across the back wall, the words, *Corruption is here. Run for your life*, were written out in blood. I thanked the Moon Goddess that Isabella had willingly stayed behind with Kylo because I didn't want her to see any of this. While I didn't like the idea of them being together, he would keep her safe, no matter the cost.

"Roman," Scarlett said, pushing me into the room and shutting the door behind me, "you made it."

"I'm not here to fool around, Scarlette. I'm looking for Derek."

She laughed in my face; evil eyes fixed on me. "Derek? He's the reason?"

"Yes."

"Oh, Romie, it's going to be a few long days, if you just wanna talk about him."

"Few days?" I asked, stepping away from her. "You have an hour."

She smirked even wider. "An hour of your time? That may be all you'll give me, but I'll take more. I have my ways with you, Alpha. I know what keeps your attention."

CHAPTER 32

KYLO

I wasn't supposed to ever feel this way about Isabella.

Sunlight flooded in through my bedroom window, fanning over Isabella's face. Bluebirds perched on the branches right outside my window and glanced in on us, chirping away like they did every morning.

When I'd marched into the Lycans' pack house, my plan was to tear Roman and her apart, so he'd be weak, and I could destroy him. It was funny how life worked like this because, now—less than two weeks later—I wanted her.

Curling my arm around her waist, I pulled her closer and inhaled her overwhelming scent of vanilla. I stuffed my nose deeper into her hair, wanting to accustom myself to her and to burn her smell into my memory forever.

Though I expected her to still be sleeping, she sucked in a breath, her smaller body tensing against mine. She readjusted herself, so her ass brushed against my throbbing cock.

I woke up hard every morning, but I hadn't had another woman in my bed, especially like this, for years now.

I exhaled deeply through my nose, trying to control myself and not wanting to overstep her boundaries. Yet she continued to tease me by arching her back, as if she were stretching, and pressing her ass harder against me.

Moon Goddess, I tried to ignore it. I really did. I thought about Roman, how we'd made up, how I didn't want to hurt him the way he'd hurt me, how—

Again, she pushed her ass against me. I inhaled the scent of her sweet, dripping cunt and curled my fingers around her waist harshly. My wolf wanted out to touch her, to see her, to claim her. And if I wasn't careful, he'd take control of me and take Isabella in the most animalistic way possible.

Instead of turning around to face me, she grabbed one of my hands, interlocked my fingers with hers, and tugged it between her breasts. After she let go, I brushed my thumb over the thin material of the T-shirt that covered her breasts, feeling the soft, tender flesh underneath. My cock swelled in my shorts, and I pressed it lightly into her.

Her breath caught in her throat, a breathy moan passing through her lips. I continued to brush my finger over her breast, each time getting closer and closer to her hard nipple that I wanted to tug on until she came.

When she pushed her hips against mine again, I flicked my thumb over her nipple. She sucked in a sharp yet quiet breath and tensed. I paused for a brief moment, feeling my wolf rave inside of me.

Control, Kylo. Control.

But she didn't want me to control myself. She bucked her hips back and forth once more, grinding her ass against my swelling cock. I grasped her breast in my hand, feeling her hard nipple press against my palm, and thrust my hips against hers, taking complete control.

She whimpered, and I did it again. Loving the sounds she made for me.

Instead of stopping me, she dug her fingernails into my thigh and arched her back even more to let my cock thrust against her pussy. Even through her underwear, I could feel how wet she was for me.

I rested my forehead on her shoulder and continued, slowly at first, but when she didn't tell me to stop, I picked up my pace and thrust my hard cock against her ass, listening to her moans fill the empty pack house.

All I wanted was to rip both of our clothes off and take her. Make her mine too.

She slipped a hand between her legs and touched her clit, rubbing herself in circles. When I pinched her nipple between my fingers, she jerked into the air with her back arching hard. I curled my hand under her thigh and pulled one of her legs into the air, giving me better access.

While she didn't say anything, I continued to pound myself against her and watched over her shoulder as she rubbed her sensitive little clit through her panties. "Fuck, *princess,*" I growled into her ear. "Just like that. Make yourself feel good for me."

Suddenly, she stiffened. I thrust against her harder, knowing that she was moments from coming. She threw her head back, legs shaking, and slapped a hand over her mouth to scream into it.

I slowed to a stop behind her, my cock so incredibly hard. I needed a fucking release.

Before I could stop myself, I rolled out of bed and mumbled a quick, "I need to use the bathroom." I rushed into the bathroom connected to my bedroom. I shut the door, placed one hand on it, pushed my other down my pants, and stroked my cock.

Imagining Isabella's pussy wrapped around it instead of my hand.

Imagining how tight she was, how she'd clench when I pounded into her.

Imagining her moaning so much, unable to stop herself.

Digging my claws into the door, I closed my eyes, came on my hand, and pretended that my cum was filling Isabella's tight little hole instead of coating my palm. It felt so fucking good; I couldn't stop myself from groaning.

After washing my hands, I sat on the closed toilet and rubbed my temples. Moon Goddess, our connection became more intense with every waking moment that I spent with her. One day, this feeling would kill me. I could just feel it.

Isabella knocked on the door and, a moment later, her fingers peeked out just beneath the door. "Kylo," she whispered.

I sat down on this side of the door and brushed my fingers under it to touch hers. "Yes, Isabella?" I asked, heart pounding in my ears.

"I think I love you."

When the words tumbled out of her mouth, I tensed. Everything slowed down, and all I could focus on was her ragged breathing on the other side of the door. My heart beat a bit faster, heat crawling up my neck. Surely, she had to be lying.

She couldn't love me.

After Scarlett had torn me to pieces, I hadn't thought that anyone could love me. Yet seconds passed, and Isabella hadn't taken it back yet.

Could it really be true? Could she really love me after spending the night together?

But when she said, "But that can't ever happen again," my chest tightened in pain.

From inside the bathroom, I heard her whisper those few

words to herself over and over again, as if she was trying to convince herself.

"Tonight, I have to sleep in another room. I ... I can't sleep with you. This can't happen."

I hesitantly opened the door to see Isabella on the ground, almost in tears. Her wolf purred, just not as loudly as she had done this morning in my bed. Doing what we had done seemed like it calmed both her and my wolf.

But the difference between our wolves was that I wanted to do it again.

Crouching down beside her, I cupped her face in my hands and drew her closer to me. She placed her hands firmly on my chest to keep me away, which felt like rejection itself. Yet my wolf couldn't deal with another rejection, so I pretended like it hadn't happened and smiled at her.

"I love you too," I whispered, tucking a strand of brown hair behind her ear. "And if you don't want that to happen again, then"—I gulped, knowing that it would be damn hard to stay away from her now that I'd had a taste—"I respect your decision."

She furrowed her brows, as if she didn't want me to say what I just had. After five minutes of sitting in complete silence, a tear fell from her eye. "You don't deserve this," she finally said. "You don't deserve to be a second choice. You deserve someone who is going to choose you time and time again."

I brushed my thumb against the corner of her lip. "I don't mind being your second choice," I said even though it killed me on the inside. I just didn't want her to leave me, not after she'd admitted that she loved me.

"I do." She grasped my face in her hands and gave me a forced, tight smile. "Maybe if I'd met you before I met Roman, things would be different, but this is how things have to be right now. I'm committed to Roman."

I laid my hands over her smaller ones and leaned into her touch. Parting my lips, I pressed them back together. I didn't know what else to say to her to get her to stay without stepping between her and Roman.

But I didn't want to try again with someone else.

"Maybe you should try to find another woman who makes you happy, someon—"

I shook my head. "No."

"But—"

"We already talked about this with the Moon Goddess, and you heard my answer."

"Kylo, I … we … this can't happen again."

"I'm happy as I am, Isabella."

"But don't you want a mate to spend your life with?"

"Goddess, I've spent centuries with you."

She playfully shoved my chest, her wolf purring for me. "I'm being serious."

"I am serious. I'm happy where I am. I haven't been with another woman for a long time, and I don't particularly want someone else right now. My pack is strong. My mom comes over to visit me every day. Things are good." Warmth spread throughout my body. "You just make them better."

"I make things better for you?" she whispered.

"You do," I whispered back, and then I leaned in and kissed her on her perfect, soft lips. "You make everything better for me."

CHAPTER 33

ISABELLA

*M*y wolf anxiously paced around inside my head, lingering close to the surface but never speaking to me once. From afar, I watched Raj train Naomi with my stomach in tight knots. This morning hadn't gone how I'd planned. I never meant to tell Kylo that I loved him. Hell, I hadn't even known I did until it came out of my mouth.

After glancing down at my phone for the fifteenth time this morning, I blew a deep breath out of my nose. Roman hadn't answered any of my calls last night or this morning. It continued to go to voice mail, and most of my texts hadn't even been delivered.

"Is everything all right?" Raj asked me from across the field. When I didn't answer, he whistled to signal for every one of the Lycans to get a drink, and then he jogged over to me. "Roman is still out, looking for Derek, isn't he?"

I tossed my phone into my bag and crossed my arms.

"He'll be okay," I said aloud, mostly for myself. I walked over to the training area, where Naomi was talking with some of the other Lycans.

No matter what happened out there with Roman, I still had responsibilities here. If we were going to win this war, I had to start training Naomi the way I did every Lycan and teach her the rules we lived by.

Fight without emotion.

Know your enemy.

Business before pleasure. Always.

"How is your experience with defensive techniques?" I asked her, tugging off my T-shirt and standing in a black sports bra and some pliable leggings in front of her. There were many things she had to learn about defensive and offensive tactics and strikes.

Naomi placed her hands on her hips. "I'm more on the offense. I don't like to be put into situations where I have to defend myself against someone stronger than me. I can do it, but I prefer to get the fight over with sooner rather than later."

I stepped toward her and tried to intimidate the human. "And what would you do if someone attacked you?" I moved closer to her, my canines lengthening from under my lips. "What would you do?"

Moving back, she analyzed my body movements. "Typically, I'd use wolfsbane against a stronger opponent. Shove a bottle of it right into their mouth to kill them instantly."

"And when you don't have the wolfsbane?" I asked as my nails lengthened into claws.

Before she could answer, I lunged at her to see how she'd react. To my surprise, she leaped back almost as quickly and immediately lowered into a fighting stance, cheeks flushing pink. Instead of lunging back at me—which most wolves did —she stayed back and let her eyes linger on my hips.

I stood back up, watching as she never took her eyes off me once, and walked over to my bag. "Trick is"—I pulled out a necklace with a tiny bottle-like pendant that had a few drops of black wolfsbane inside of it, and I tossed it to her —"always have wolfsbane on you."

"This is wolfsbane?" she asked, tilting the pendant to the side and staring at how the few droplets moved inside the bottle. "Will this kill a wolf instantly? I usually use more."

"The wolfsbane that most packs have weaponized is diluted, so they can buy more of it at a cheaper price," Raj said, pointing to the necklace. "That's the real thing. Don't go using it on just anyone unless you're in danger that you cannot get out of. Otherwise, fight."

A cold summer breeze drifted through the forest, making the hairs on my arm stand straight. I looked at Raj. "Work on her defense for today. In the meantime, I'll find a witch who uses corrupt magic similar to Dolus's. We can have them use their magic against Naomi, so she can build up her resistance."

Us wolves could build some of our resistance, too, but we didn't have as much mental strength compared to humans, and magic required so much mental capacity. While were-wolves were physically strong and brave and courageous, we acted off of pure, animalistic instinct. Naomi—and other humans like her—could resist that innate, wolfish urge to kill ruthlessly, instead thinking a situation through before attacking.

After Raj nodded, I sat at the edge of the field and scrolled through my list of Contacts for anyone who might have relations with witches. Every so often, I glanced up at the Lycans who hadn't practiced late last night, watching them practice now. Even Kylo practiced with some of the stronger wolves today, yet my wolf wasn't really bothered by the way every one of his muscles flexed with ease as he fought mercilessly.

All she could think about was Roman.

So, I called him again. His phone rang and rang and rang and then went to voice mail.

I sighed deeply through my nose, trying not to be too upset, and scanned through more of my Contacts. There weren't many witches or sorcerers around this part of the forest, but there had to be a couple. When I found a few people who *might know someone,* I sent their contact information to Raj's phone.

What scared me the most about this entire ordeal was that we had a mole in Roman's pack—someone who'd helped kidnap Derek—and whoever it was seemed perfectly healthy. It could be Derek himself or Vanessa or even Roman.

After an entire day and a half without hearing from Roman, I sat across from Vanessa at The Night Raider's Café. Though dark and stormy outside, the coffee shop was bustling with people picking pine needles out of their wet hair and shaking off the rain.

Vanessa had basically dragged me here, telling me that I couldn't just stay in the house and sulk all night. My knee bounced under the table as I glanced at my phone every other minute, hoping that Roman would call me. We were too far apart for the mind link to work.

Neither my wolf nor I liked that we couldn't contact our mate. It reminded us of all those late nights when we'd lain in bed at the Lycans' pack house, wondering if Roman was okay without us—because we weren't okay without him.

My phone lit up.

Raj: Just finished practice with Naomi. It's only been a couple days, but she's made significant advances in her fighting skills. I've contacted some of the witches and

sorcerers. I'm waiting to hear back and preparing her mentally until then. Have a good night. Contact me if you need me.

I pushed my discouraging thoughts away and told myself that if Roman were in danger, he'd call me to help him. But Roman was the dominant, do-it-all-myself type of alpha. Part of me believed that he wouldn't even *want* my help in trying to defeat his ex-girlfriend and finding Derek.

Vanessa wiped some strawberry ice cream off my fingers, which had dripped down from my cone. "Come on, Isabella. Relax," she said to me. "Why have you been so worried these past two days?"

I licked the ice cream. "Roman went to find Scarlett."

She slammed her hand onto the table, her bronze rings clattering against the wood. "What the fuck? I told him to stay away from her."

"When did you tell him that?"

"A couple weeks ago." She scratched the back of her neck and looked at the flickering decorative candle between us. "I wanted him to know that if he doesn't take care of you, then someone else will." She quieted her voice to almost a whisper. "Just looking out for a friend."

After leaning forward on my elbows, I grabbed her wrist. "Thank you."

She grinned back at me, rested her elbows against the table, and leaned closer as she licked her plain vanilla cone. My lips curled into a smile at the thought of her actually not being shitty to me anymore. So much had changed since I became a Lycan, and this change was one I could get behind.

"What're you smiling like that for?" she asked, tugging on a strand of my hair.

"It feels so good to be able to be with you like this," I said honestly. To be able to laugh and be happy, to have a friend I could lean on when I felt like my world was crashing down on me.

Suddenly, Vanessa leaned over the table and kissed me.

My eyes widened, and I tensed, unable to comprehend what was even happening. I tore myself away from her and swallowed in both fear and confusion. Had Vanessa just kissed me?

Vanessa pulled away with fearful eyes. "Isabella, I'm so sorry. I-I didn't mean to. I thought that … that you …" She rubbed her hand over the front of her neck, skin turning a bright red.

I stood and accidentally crushed my ice cream cone in my fist. "I have to go," I said, tossing it in the garbage and hurrying toward the exit of the café. My mind was in a fog, thoughts running rampant through my head. "I have to go."

Wind whipped rain around the forest like a damn tornado. I shifted into my wolf and sprinted into the woods, my paws sinking into the mud. These past few days just kept getting crazier. Roman had been gone for two days, I had confessed my undying love for a man who I had apparently shared seven-thousand years with, and Vanessa had kissed me.

Kissed me.

With everything going on, part of me feared that *I* was the corrupted one who was slowly going mad. I started for Kylo's pack house with tears in my eyes at the thought of doing something so intimate without Roman's permission.

Roman had told me that I could do anything but sex with Kylo … but Vanessa?

"Need mate," my wolf whimpered. *"Roman."*

I leaped over the gorge and collapsed on the other side, scraping my thigh against a jagged rock hard enough to draw blood. If I had known that Vanessa was into me, I wouldn't have treated her any different because she had been such a really good friend lately, but I just … wished it'd never happened.

When Kylo's pack house came into view, I transformed back into my human and draped one of his shirts he had stuffed in his foyer's closet over my body. Kylo appeared in the hallway in nothing but a pair of sweats.

"What's wrong?" he asked.

I hurried to him and hugged my arms around his body. *What was wrong?* So much was wrong. I didn't know where to start. I wanted to be strong. I wanted to be so strong. But being without Roman had made me so weak, both physically and mentally.

As I doubled over into him, tears burst from my eyes.

Kylo picked me up, walked to the couch, and sat me on his lap. "What's wrong, Isabella?" he asked, peeling my hands away from my face. "Please tell me, so I know how to make it better."

"Derek is missing. Dolus is coming. Vanessa just kissed me. And I miss Roman." I sobbed into his shirt.

He ran his fingers through my hair, trying to soothe me, and pressed his lips to my temple.

"Has he called you?" I asked desperately.

I needed him to be alive. What if he hadn't called because Scarlett had corrupted him? What if, when he came home, he wasn't the same? My heart tightened. I just wanted my mate back in my arms.

"I've tried contacting him multiple times, but I haven't reached him."

"Do you think he's okay? Do you think he's alive?"

"He's alive, Isabella."

"What if he isn't?" I whispered. I tucked my head into the crook of his neck and closed my eyes, hoping that sleep would make all my problems go away just for a few hours. "What if my mate is dead?"

CHAPTER 34

ISABELLA

*C*urled into Kylo's bare chest, I blinked my eyes open to see the outline of a man in the darkness. He sat at the edge of the bed, one of his hands on my leg under the blankets as he talked to Kylo. I inhaled a whiff of mint deeply and jumped into Roman's arms.

Legs wrapped around his waist, face stuffed into the crook of his neck, fingers thrust through his thick brown hair, I held him so tightly to me and murmured his name against my mark. "I missed you so much."

Roman chuckled lowly in my ear and wrapped his arms around me. Scarlett's scent lingered faintly in his hair, but I let it slide because all that mattered at this moment was that my mate was home safely.

After kissing my forehead, Roman pulled away from me and rested his hands on my hips. "We need to talk."

Glancing between him and Kylo, I nodded and felt a bit guilty for everything that had happened between

Kylo and me *and* between Vanessa and me when Roman was gone. "Please, let me go first," I said. Yet when I opened my mouth, nothing came out, except, "Kylo and I …"

Roman tensed. "Did you … have sex?"

"No," I reassured him. "But we—"

Almost immediately, Roman blew out a relieved breath. "Then, I don't want to hear what you did," he said.

I shifted uncomfortably under his intense stare and wondered why he didn't want to know that we had … we had touched each other and then confessed our love.

He cleared his throat, his unreadable gaze flickering to Kylo. "Not yet."

I glanced between them, trying to understand the expression they had just exchanged, but dropped decided not to ask them about it when Roman grabbed my hand and led me to the living room. Kylo followed and sat on a leather love seat across from us.

"Wait," I said, placing a hand on Roman's chest. "I have to tell you something else."

Roman furrowed his brows, patience in his eyes slipping, yet he took a deep breath and brushed a piece of hair off my cheek. "What is it, Isabella?"

"Vanessa kissed me."

Angry, possessive dominance dripped from every one of his features, which made me even more confused. How was he angry with Vanessa for kissing me but didn't want to know what I had done with Kylo, which was much, much worse?

"Why?" he asked.

"I have no idea! We were just having ice cream, and she kissed me."

"Did you like it?" he asked.

"No! I pushed her away," I said. "Are you … mad?"

After pausing for a few moments, he clenched his jaw. "A little, yes. *At her.*"

I stared at him with wide eyes. My guarded Roman *rarely* talked about his emotions. It was … refreshing beyond belief to hear him speak so honestly and openly about what he thought.

"But you're not angry with Kylo?" I asked to be clear.

"I gave you permission to stay with Kylo, Isabella. I knew what was going to happen between you two. I had been thinking about it since the moment you told me you were mates. I trusted you not to have sex with him, and you didn't." He glanced over at Kylo, who nodded. "I know that this connection you have with him is something that makes you strong. I know that this"—he looked between Kylo and me—"was going to happen sooner or later. And I wanted it to be on my terms. I didn't want you to go behind my back."

My stomach tightened. "Are you sure?"

"Yes," Roman reassured, rubbing circles on my knee. "Kylo knows what I will allow and what I will not allow you to do together *when I'm not here*, just like you know my limits too." His eyes shimmered gold. "Whatever goes on between you and him is your choice. I'm asking for something simple, considering our relationship. I don't like to share what is mine, but if it makes you stronger and helps us communicate, then that's what it has to be like for now."

I pressed my lips together, searching his eyes for any sort of doubt. Yet there was none.

He smiled at me, his eyes drifting to my lips. "I have always given you a choice, Isabella." He brushed his finger against my bottom lip. "I have never held you back from something great, have never stopped you from doing whatever you wanted."

My heart tightened at the thought of my possessive alpha mate being so considerate. Since the beginning, Roman had sacrificed so much for me: he had given me a choice to be his mate by waiting until I was eighteen to understand our bond, he had let me go to the Lycans without stopping me because it was important to me, and now, he was letting my wolf connect with Kylo.

Kylo brushed his hand against my knee and smiled. "If it makes you feel more comfortable, we can start by being friends," he said.

But both he and I knew that we could never be *just friends* after what had happened the other morning.

After a few moments, Roman nodded to Kylo. "How was everything?"

As they dived into a conversation, I relaxed in Roman's arms, rested my head in his lap, and let him brush his hand against my hair. It was odd that after Kylo had come into the picture, Roman and I had been more intimate too. The old Roman—the one I had fallen in love with years ago—had come back.

Staring between Kylo and Roman, I smiled.

Our mates are safe, my wolf said.

She said the word *mates* like we had mated with both of them already. I closed my eyes, content with how this was all working out in such a weird way. And now that Roman was home, my wolf would hopefully be less angsty around Kylo for a bit.

Around four a.m., Roman picked me up. "You can't fall back asleep yet, Isabella."

"I know," I said, yawning. "We have to run home."

"You'll stay here tonight," Kylo said.

"In your spare room?" I asked as Roman walked with me down the hallway, passing every spare room in this pack house.

When Kylo pushed open his bedroom door, Roman walked into the room and placed me on the bed.

"In Kylo's bed?" I asked with wide eyes. "I don't know if this is a good idea."

Roman lay on his side next to me, resting his head on his hand, and stared down at me. The moonlight bounced off of his hazel eyes and illuminated his tired, stressed face. He brushed a finger up the center of my chest. "We're staying here for tonight, but we have other things to talk about." He grasped my chin in his hand. "Like what you and Kylo did the other morning."

"I thought you said that you didn't want to know."

"I said that I didn't want to know *yet*," he said, eyes tinting gold the way they always did before he forced me down onto my knees.

I looked at Kylo, who sat at the end of the bed, passionate brown eyes fixed on me. I should've fucking known that they had been up to something all this time.

Roman grabbed my chin. "You didn't think I didn't want to know at all, did you?"

"Um …"

Completely awake now, I parted my lips and pressed them back together. Heat slithered up my body, making me hot *everywhere* but especially between my legs. I pulled my knees to my chest, nipples hardening under their intense stares.

Roman tucked some hair behind my ear. "Oh, it's okay, Isabella. You don't have to tell me. You can show me," he said, pushing me onto my side. He lay behind me with his cock against my ass and his hand stuffed between my legs.

My breath caught in the back of my throat, my mouth dry. "I …"

Did he really want me to show him exactly what Kylo and I had done while Kylo was right in front of us?

"This?" Roman asked, finger dragging my oversize T-shirt up my legs.

At the edge of the bed, Kylo gazed at my thighs, pressed his lips together, and took an unsteady breath through his nose. His usual soft brown eyes were a vehement gold, burning into every inch of my flesh that he hadn't *really* touched yet.

I shook my head. "No," I whispered. "Not this."

Roman lifted one of my legs into the air and let Kylo see my gray cloth underwear, soaked with my arousal. After played with my entrance, he slipped his fingers into me easily. "This?" he asked.

When I shook my head, Roman growled low into my ear and thrust his bulge against my pussy. "What about like this?"

I pressed my legs together and only let out a small whimper. Kylo had thrust against me over and over and over the other morning, his cock throbbing against his underwear and my pussy wet with anticipation. All my wolf had wanted in that moment was for him to stick himself in me raw and fuck me until I begged him to stop.

"He touched you like this, didn't he?" Roman asked, continuing to thrust against me.

"Yes," I whispered as my pussy clenched.

Roman ripped my panties right off of me, leaving my bare pussy glistening under the moonlight.

Kylo glanced between my legs and pressed his hand against the bulge in his gray sweatpants. "Fuck," he breathed out, fingers moving so slowly down every inch of his cock.

I squirmed slightly in Roman's hold, the pressure between my legs almost unbearable even though neither one of them had really touched me yet. But that didn't stop my wolf from thinking about everything two domineering alphas could do to me in the bedroom.

"I bet you wanted to do more with him," Roman said. "I bet you wanted this …" He plunged his fingers into my pussy and pumped in and out, sending a wave of pleasure through my body.

Unable to hold myself back, I grasped his wrist, arched my back, and rode his fingers like a carnal beast trapped in heat, desperate to come.

When he pulled out his fingers, I whined, "Please, Roman. Put them back."

Roman chuckled against me. "I have something better for you." He pulled out his cock and slapped it against my entrance, slipping just the head inside of me. "I bet you wanted this too," he said, and in one swift movement, he shoved all of himself inside me.

Gripping the bedsheets, I clenched around him. "Oh Goddess …"

Heat gathered in my core as Roman slowly pumped in and out of me, forcing me to listen to the sloppy noises my pussy made for him. I closed my eyes to try to even my shaky breathing and displace all the tension. Yet after a few strokes, Roman showed no signs of stopping. Instead, he tugged me on top of him with my back against his chest and rested my feet on his thighs, giving Kylo a clear view of what was Roman's.

Kylo stroked his huge cock through his pants. I stared down at it with wide eyes and imagined how I'd feel if he pulled all eight inches of himself out, wrapped his hand around it, and stroked himself in front of me.

"Tell me what you *wanted* Kylo to do to you," Roman said into my ear.

I shook my head, unable to admit it out loud, especially to Roman.

Roman pumped faster into me and rubbed my clit in furious little circles. "If you're not going to tell me what you wanted the other morning, then tell me what you want him to do to you now."

Sucking in a sharp breath, I said, "Nothing. I … I don't want him to do anything to me."

"But you're clenching," Roman asked in my ear, making me clench even harder around him. "You must want something."

Don't think about it, Isabella. Don't think about Kylo ram—

"Isabella, if this is going to work, you need to be able to communicate." Roman continued to thrust into my pussy, getting his cock wet with my juices. "Now, one last chance, what do you want Kylo to do to you?"

Though I wanted to scream out every sinful thing that I wanted Kylo to do to me, I didn't want to hurt Roman. So, I kept my mouth shut and let my pussy pulse on his cock as Kylo slipped a hand into his pants.

Roman growled in my ear, "You're really going to make me punish you in front of Kylo, aren't you?" he asked me harshly. He grabbed my breasts in both his hands and tugged hard on my nipples.

Pain mixed with sheer, undeniable pleasure rushed through me. My entire body felt like it was on fire, like I was going into heat yet I had my mate with me this time. Electricity shot up and down my arms and legs, making them tingle.

When I answered Roman with a mere whimper, he pulled his cock out of my pussy, repositioned himself near my ass, and shoved himself into my tight hole, still squeezing my nipples. Then, he growled at Kylo, "Eat her pussy."

Goddess … did Roman just—

I tried to close my legs, but Kylo had already maneuvered himself between them with his warm breath fanning my clit. I squeezed my eyes closed, a wave of pleasure crashing over my body. He brushed his fingers up the insides of my thighs and lifted them into the air, resting them on his shoulders.

And then, finally, he pressed his lips onto my clit, his tongue immediately lapping at it.

"Oh Goddess," I moaned, squirming in their hold.

Roman brushed his teeth against his mark. "Watch him," he grunted.

"No."

After I defied him for the last time tonight, Roman curled his arms around my legs, hooked his hands behind my head so I was in a full Nelson position, and forced me to stare down at Kylo. Face buried between my legs, Kylo massaged my clit in torturous circles with his tongue and pushed two fingers inside of me.

"*Princess*, you're so tight and warm," Kylo said.

I clenched around both him and Roman at the mere pressure of my holes being filled. But what if ... what if it were Kylo's cock instead of his fingers, disappearing between my pussy lips and pounding into me at the same feral rhythm that Roman was?

"Still nothing, Isabella?" Roman asked low in my ear. "You don't want anything more?"

Swallowing hard, I stared down at Kylo with my heart racing inside my chest. "No," I said, the word coming out in a raspy whimper.

Yet they both knew that was a lie. Neither my wolf nor I wanted *just this*. We wanted more.

"He's going to punish you for lying," Roman said, thrusting even deeper into my ass.

I sucked in a deep breath, the pressure in my core rising.

Punish me? How was Kylo going to punish me?

"Tell him to tug on your sensitive nipples."

A wave of pleasure rolled through me. I gazed down at Kylo, brows furrowed. "Tug on my nipples," I said breathlessly.

Kylo pulled his fingers out of me and reached up with

both hands to play with my tits and roll my nipples around his palms. When he tugged on them, I arched my back and moaned so loudly that it echoed through the empty house.

"Harder," Roman said in my ear.

"Harder," I told Kylo. He did as I'd said and yanked on them. "Harder."

Kylo groaned at my demand, as if being dominated made him as hard as him dominating someone. He licked my clit faster. My pussy pulsed, just aching for something to be inside of it now that Kylo's fingers were gone.

"Tell him why you're making him do this to you, Isabella," Roman said.

"Because … because … I need to be punished."

"Why?"

Goddess, I just needed Kylo to shove his cock into me.

"Because I've been a bad girl."

Roman brushed his nose against his mark. "And what have you done that's worth punishment?"

"I lied," I whispered.

Kylo pinched my nipples harder, and I arched my back, screaming to the high heavens and trying to squirm away from him because the tension was too much to handle. My legs trembled on Kylo's shoulders.

"Don't fucking come yet," Roman growled. "We're not finished with you."

"I lied about not wanting Kylo to touch me. I want him to touch me more," I admitted.

"I don't want to hear what you want anymore, Isabella. *Tell* him what to do to you."

My eyes widened slightly as Kylo sucked my clit between his lips, tugged on it gently, and sat up between my legs. His cock was hard against his briefs and looked so fucking huge.

All I wanted was for him to … "Take them off," I said, staring at his pants.

The things I would do just to see his cock that hard.

Kylo slowly pulled off his pants and underwear, his cock springing out, and tossed them off the bed. My core pulsed, aching for it to slide into my wet pussy, stretch me out, and pound into me raw at Roman's feral pace. Instead, he placed one hand on my thigh and another around the base of his cock, stroking it inches from my pussy.

So close. It was so fucking close.

"Tell him what you want," Roman murmured into my ear.

Roman was serious about this whole relationship. He wanted it to happen on his terms, and this was his terms. When he had come over, he had probably known that he was going to take me in Kylo's bed and let him join.

After I licked my dry lips, I shook my head in defiance. "No."

Roman growled and rubbed two of his fingers against my swollen clit. "Was that punishment not enough for you, my dear Isabella?"

"It wasn't enough," I said, knowing that it would rile him up.

He moved his fingers faster as Kylo continued to trail his fingertips up and down my inner thigh.

I snarled, "Matter of fact, it sucked. I could've—"

Roman wrapped a hand around my neck. "Put your cock down this pretty little throat of hers," he said to Kylo, strumming his fingers up the column of my throat. "She won't be able to backtalk then."

My eyes widened, my pussy quivering. Kylo crawled up the bed toward me, grasped my chin in his hand, and forced me to stare up at him. From all those snide comments, I knew that he wanted me to be the dominant one in bed, could tell how good it'd felt for him when I told him to tug on my nipples, but he was an alpha … and somewhere deep down inside of him, he didn't like being defied either.

"Do it," I taunted him. "You won—"

Before I could finish, he stuffed his cock into my hot mouth and made me to wrap my lips around it. And when he hit the back of my throat, I gagged.

"Come on, Isabella." Roman continued to rub my clit. "You can take more of his cock inside of you." He tightened his hand around my throat. "If you can take all of me, you can take all of him."

Kylo thrust his cock deeper into my mouth, hitting the back of my throat again.

"Tell him you want it deeper," Roman said into my ear.

I parted my lips to speak but couldn't get any words out. My eyes watered as I stared up at Kylo's taut body, all the muscles and those soul-piercing gold eyes. I lifted my head to take more of him into my throat until my lips pressed against his hips.

"All of him, Isabella." Roman tightened his hand around my throat even more, feeling Kylo's cock all the way down it.

I took a deep breath through my nose, closed my eyes, and pressed myself closer to his hips. I wrapped my hand around the base of his cock and his balls, parted my lips even more, and forced *all* of him in my mouth.

My throat felt full, and I couldn't breathe, yet Kylo was groaning in pleasure.

Goddess, it felt so good, being able to please both of my mates.

When I needed to breathe, I pulled back slightly, but Roman held me in place. "You're not going to move until you're ready to tell Kylo everything you want him to do to you. Do you understand me?"

I nodded my head, eyes filling with tears and spit rolling down my chin.

"Answer him," Kylo said finally.

Staring up at him through my lashes, I tried to answer

him but could only gag more on my own spit. I pushed Kylo deeper down my throat, wrapped my hand around my neck to feel him inside of me, and jerked Kylo off in my throat.

Almost like an innate reflex, he jerked his cock deeper. My tits bounced against the backs of his thighs as Roman pounded up into my ass. I spread my legs for him, letting him play with my pussy folds.

I pulled away slowly, but Roman stopped me again.

"Are you ready to finally tell him?" he asked, and I nodded.

When Kylo pulled out of me, wads of spit dripped from his cock onto my chin.

I gasped for air, and with watery eyes, I looked right up at him. "Fuck me, please." I snatched his chin in my hand. "Fuck me hard, Kylo—as hard as you wanted to fuck me the other morning—and don't fucking stop until I'm coming all over your cock."

He let out a low, lascivious growl and crawled between my legs.

Roman pulled them further apart and sucked my earlobe between his lips. "That wasn't hard, was it?" he asked.

Before Kylo could thrust into me, I pressed my heel into his hip. "Spit on my pussy first, Kylo. Make it even wetter for you, so your cock slips right in."

Roman tensed behind me, the way he always did when he was close to coming.

Kylo spit on my pussy and rubbed it in with his fingers, and then in one slow thrust, he pushed himself inside of me. My whole body tingled with pleasure. Every inch of him drove me higher and higher. I had never been filled by two huge cocks before, never had this much pleasure and pressure surging through my body.

Roman grabbed the backs of my thighs and spread me

wide. I arched my back, loving the feeling of two cocks pumping in and out of my holes.

"Touch me, Kylo," I whimpered. "Rub my clit."

Brows furrowed in delight, Kylo rubbed my clit and pumped into me.

Roman wrapped one hand around my throat to pull me closer and sucked on his mark. "Is that all you want, my dear Isabella?" he asked me, fingers dancing up the column of my neck.

For once, I decided to obey him and shook my head.

"Then, tell me what you want."

"I want to ride Kylo while you pound into me from behind."

Kylo pulled out, lay on the bed, and tugged me on top of him, so I straddled his waist. When he positioned himself at my entrance, I interlocked my fingers with his, slowly slid down on his cock, and moaned into his mouth.

After positioning himself behind me, Roman curled his hands around my throat and slammed himself into my ass again. He tugged on my hair to force my head back and then kissed me from above. Kylo dipped his hand between my legs and rubbed my clit like I had told him to earlier. I dug my fingers into his chest, feeling all the tense muscles.

"Come inside of me, Roman," I moaned against Roman's lips. "Please, come inside of me."

Roman thrust hard and fast into me, and then suddenly, he stilled, his warm and thick cum filling my ass. His body trembled behind me, hips jerking further toward me. He grasped my ass and pressed his lips hard to mine.

When Roman pulled out, I was teetering on the edge of an orgasm. He captured my nipples between his fingers and tugged on them hard. I screamed out his name, my pussy pulsing on Kylo's cock, and collapsed into his arms.

Kylo held me down onto him, continued to thrust up into

me, and let me come all over him. When I finished, I slowly crawled off of him and back between his legs, my breasts brushing against his thighs. His cock, wet with my juices, sprang back against his abdomen.

I stroked him hard and fast, staring up into his golden eyes. "You're going to come when I tell you to," I told Kylo.

His hips jerked into the air, cock twitching. I placed my lips right on his head, swirled my tongue around it, and massaged his balls lightly.

And when I knew that he wouldn't last any longer, I took all of him into my mouth until he hit the back of my throat. "Come for me, Kylo," I managed to get out.

Almost immediately, he filled my throat with his warm cum and groaned. I swallowed his cum, sat up between his legs, and collapsed between him and Roman.

It had been a long, surprising night.

"Get some rest, Isabella," Roman said. "We'll talk about Scarlett in the morning."

CHAPTER 35

ROMAN

*T*he next morning, I woke up, lying on my back in Kylo's bed. Bluebirds sat on the windowsill, flapped their wings, and chirped. Isabella curled into my chest as Kylo spooned her, his nose in her hair, like mine usually was.

When I had come here last night, I hadn't known that we'd end up like this. I had spent two entire days with that annoying bitch Scarlett and needed to relax, and Isabella had looked too damn sexy with that bedhead to pass up.

While sharing wasn't what normal mated wolves did, my wolf was oddly content with how it had played out so far. Isabella wasn't going behind my back and hadn't done anything I'd told her not to do. This had happened on *my* terms, and our communication had been better than ever.

Kylo curled his fingers into Isabella's hips, his knuckles brushing against my abdomen. I shifted in the bed toward Isabella and closed my eyes, hoping to get a few more moments of sleep before I had to torture Scarlett for any more information.

Suddenly, Isabella shot up in the bed. Startled, the blue-birds flew away and into the nearest tree, perching on a branch but still staring into the room.

Isabella scrambled out of the bed and tugged on one of Kylo's shirts. "Where is he? Where's Derek? That should've been the first goddess-damned thing I asked you when you got back." She paced around the room, shaking her head. "What the hell is wrong with me?"

Kylo blinked open his eyes and grabbed her hand to tug her back down. "Come back to bed. It's six in the morning. We got less than two hours of sleep."

After pulling her hand out of his, Isabella turned to me, nipples hard under that shirt. "We need to talk." When she moved her arms over her chest, I looked back up at her face. "Now," she said. "Where's Derek?"

Knowing that she wouldn't even try to get any more sleep, I sat up in bed. Being a Lycan had fucked with her sleep schedule too much. If she got an hour of sleep at night, she had way too much energy.

"Scarlett is in my prison, being tortured by guards until she gives us information," I said. A wave of guilt washed over me at the thought of spending two restless nights without Isabella and having to come home empty-handed. "I didn't find Derek."

Isabella threw her hands up in the air and started mumbling to herself—or maybe her wolf—something about controlling herself around us, so she could find him. "Why didn't you tell me this last night, Roman? I could've gone out and—"

"Because Kylo told me you had been on edge for the past two days and were a mess when you got home last night," I said, eyes hardening at her.

She might've been physically, mentally, and emotionally strong, but we were just wolves after all. We weren't gods, and we couldn't do it all without rest and without thinking clearly. If I had told Isabella, she would've blindly run out into those woods, not caring who or what kind of corruption was out there.

"You still should've told me," she said. "He's my best friend."

Kylo leaned against the headboard next to me, staying quiet. While he might've come off as that loud, rude alpha during the alphas meeting, I had always known him to keep to himself. If it wasn't his problem, he didn't typically speak up about it.

I crawled out of the bed and placed my hands on her muscular shoulders. "I didn't want you to freak out like this. You need to sleep. You can't keep yourself up all night, especially when Dolus is out there, corrupting minds." I grabbed her hands. "Beating yourself up over it isn't going to make it better. I tried that when my mom died, and nothing changed."

"But," she said in a quiet voice, "I could be trying to find him."

"The only person who knows where he is, is Scarlett," Kylo said.

"And Scarlett isn't talking. She won't talk. I have tried everything," I admitted.

Brows furrowed together, Isabella looked at me with big eyes. "Everything?"

"Not that," I said, knowing that she thought the absolute worst after catching Scarlett flirting with me at the Lycans' over a week ago.

But I didn't blame Isabella. She had a lot on her mind, and Scarlett was corrupt as hell right now.

She'd do anything to tear us apart and taint us too.

Isabella looked over at Kylo. "Can you try talking to her?"

"She's not going to tell me anything," Kylo said. "She hates me for rejecting her."

Isabella let out a low growl and pulled on a pair of sweatpants. "Then, I'm going to kick the shit out of her until she tells me where my best friend is," she said, hurrying to the door.

I caught her by the wrist before she could leave. "You're not going to see her. She's going to play mind games with you. She knows that Derek being gone is hurting you. She'll fuck with your mind like she did to whoever helped her escape with Derek."

"I don't care if she *tries* to fuck with my head. I'm going to get Derek back whether—"

"I'll go," Kylo interrupted, scooching out of the bed. He put on a pair of tight jeans and a gray V-neck. "I'll talk to her, see what I can get out of her." He slid an arm around her waist. "Roman will find the mole. You go train Naomi."

Still unsatisfied with both of us, she crossed her arms. "On one condition: a Lycan accompanies each of you today because I'm not going to allow either of you to be corrupted." She lowered her voice and unfolded her arms. "Especially not now, not after last night."

I grasped her chin, pulled her toward me, and kissed her. "Deal."

It had been fucking hours of listening to everyone in my pack say the same shit about not knowing Derek had been taken. Some people were crying, and others were hysterical about corruption taking over this pack.

"Roman," Isabella's mother said, touching my shoulder and smiling down softly at me, "you have a lot of responsibility right now. Isabella told us what was happening. If you need—"

"Meatloaf," Isabella's dad said with a huge grin.

"A cooked meal," Isabella's mom said, narrowing her eyes at her mate, "you're always welcome at our house." She leaned in close and covered her mouth with her hand. "We all know his meatloaf is the worst."

Isabella's dad arched a brow. "What was that, honey?"

She smiled at him and waved her hand. "Oh, nothing, sweetie."

I walked them to my office door. "Thank you."

After they disappeared down the hallway, I rubbed my hand over my face and groaned. This was beyond tiring. I didn't want to believe that any one of these people had aided and abetted Dolus and Scarlett. Every one of my packmates treated me better than family, especially after Mom and Dad died.

Cayden walked into my office and sat on one of the chairs, kicking one leg over the other. As I was about to shut the door to talk with him, Jane wandered down the hallway, humming a song Mom used to sing.

"Jane," I said, sighing through my nose. This morning, I had told her to go home, where she would be safe, for the entire day. I didn't want her roaming around the pack when someone had just kidnapped one of my most valuable warriors like it was nothing. "Please go back to your house, lock yourself inside of it, and don't answer the door for anyone. I can't risk you getting hurt."

She hummed to herself, muttered something about how I was annoying and too restrictive under her breath, and walked out of the pack house. I ran my hands through my hair and gazed back over at Cayden, who was scrolling on his phone.

Since Cayden was my beta *and* my strongest warrior, I

didn't think that he was the rat, but someone close to me had to have known that Jane was being watched. He had known it the moment that I assigned Derek to her.

Cayden grimaced at me. "What'd you want to talk about?"

"Did you find any information about Derek?" I asked.

"No. I couldn't get anything out of Scarlett last night. She sat in her cell, completely content, like she thought that someone was going to let her out." Cayden grimaced. "She's terrifying as fuck, if you ask me. I don't know why you ever dated her."

I rolled my eyes. She hadn't always been that way.

"And you didn't see anyone unusual around the property?" I asked.

"No," he said, narrowing his eyes at me. "Why?"

"That's all," I said, ignoring his question. I waved him off.

After lingering for a few moments, Cayden sighed and left the room.

When he closed the door behind him, I nodded to Isabella's Lycan warrior. I had to be sure that it wasn't him. "Follow Cayden."

CHAPTER 36

KYLO

*J*t took me the entire day to get the courage to talk to Scarlett for the first time in years. After I'd found her with Roman four years ago, I'd vowed I wouldn't speak with her unless I had gained the strength to sever our mate bond for good. And when I finally had, I hadn't turned back.

Somehow though, she had managed to weasel her way back between Roman and me, except this time, she couldn't tear us apart because neither one of us wanted or cared about her like that anymore.

"Kylo," Scarlett purred as I shuffled down the stone steps into the dungeon. She sat with her back against the wall, silver metal bounding and burning into her wrists and ankles. "I never thought I'd see you and Roman be *civil.*"

I leaned against the wall, crossed my arms over my chest, and stared at the woman I'd once called *mate and luna.*

Though I wanted to say I felt nothing for her, I still ached because of what she had done. It was unforgivable betrayal.

"Tell me where Derek is," I said.

Scarlett tossed her brown hair over her shoulder. "Why don't you go ask your lover?"

Overcome with anger, I stepped forward and grabbed the silver bars. "Are you still fucking angry about Isabella and me? If you hadn't slept with Roman behind my back, maybe you wouldn't be sitting in an empty, cold cell. Things could've been different."

They might have been different between us, but I still would've felt the same way about Isabella. We had been fated to be together for seven thousand years and found each other again and again in our past lives.

Fuck Scarlett and what she had done to me.

She wasn't the woman I needed. Isabella was.

"Why do you care that I slept with him?" she asked through her canines and stood. "You knew that we had been flirting. We did it in front of you! Why wouldn't I sleep with him? His dick is so much bigger than yours, Kylo … and all that pure, raw dominance"—she snickered—"you have none of it."

I released the silver bars and took a deep breath. She wouldn't get to me.

"It's not that you slept with him. It's that you broke my trust. It's that you slept with him in my bedroom and in every single room in my pack house." I breathed deeply through my nose, repeating to myself that this was another one of her many mind games.

Her lips curled into a cruel smirk. "I don't regret it. He was the best time I ever had."

Kill her, my wolf growled. *End her, so she can't cause any more pain.*

Instead of hurling my fists at her, I clenched them by my

sides. No matter how hard I tried, she wouldn't give me any kind of information about Derek. She would run me in circles until I crumpled beneath her.

I walked out of the prison to keep my sanity; her whines being drowned out through the thick concrete doors. I headed straight toward the pack house, on a mission to find Isabella to get my mind off Scarlett.

Yet Scarlett always had a way of getting to me, even after I had rejected her.

CHAPTER 37

ISABELLA

*T*welve hours on my feet, training Naomi, organizing the Lycans, and contacting a witch competent in corruption magic, I rested my forehead against Roman's pack house front door and blew out a deep breath. I hadn't found shit about Derek's whereabouts and wasn't closer to finding the mole.

When I walked into the house, Roman and Kylo were talking tensely with each other at the kitchen table. There was a notebook between them with a dozen words listed down the side of it in bright red ink.

"What's that?" I asked.

Kylo smiled at me. "A list of a hundred things we want to do with you later."

I cocked my brow at him and then at Roman, who had a small smirk on his face and playful hazel eyes. Sitting beside Kylo, I snatched the notebook and read all the names from it, humming to myself.

"You want all these people *to do* me later?" I asked, unable to suppress my smile. "Vanessa, Cayden, even Raj. You two are a pair of kinky mother—"

Roman's playful eyes hardened as he tore the notebook away from me. "Now that you've had a taste of Kylo, don't push it," he said. He shut the notebook and placed his pen on top of it, sliding it to the other side of the table. "Those are names of people who could have helped Scarlett out."

After taking my hand from across the table, Roman drew his fingers over my knuckles. "I have a couple of the Lycans watching them," he said. "No need to worry. I'm not trusting many people here. Whoever it was had to be someone close to us if they knew that Derek was watching Jane. I only told my closest warriors about it."

I turned toward Kylo. "And Scarlett?"

Kylo blew out a breath and sank in his chair, shaking his head. "She won't talk to me. All she did was run me around in circles. She's not one to give in easily. Even after all the torture that your guards put her through, she seemed so damn calm." He frowned at me. "I'll try again tomorrow, but I don't think she's going to say anything."

We sat in silence for a few moments, and then I picked up an apple from the center of the table. "Well, I just wanted to check in. I'll be back home later," I said, standing back up and starting for the door.

The witch had made plans to come to the Lycans' later tonight to aid us, and I wanted to get there a bit early to prepare Naomi.

Kylo clutched my wrist and pulled me back to the table. "Where are you going?"

"I have a meeting with a few Lycans tonight at seven. It's almost six thirty."

"I didn't dismiss you," Roman said.

"Dismiss me?" I asked, brow raised. "You don't have to dismiss me."

Kylo stood up and snaked his hand around the front of my throat, his nose in my hair, lips against my ear. "Sit."

I inhaled his sweet pine scent and closed my eyes, waiting for Roman to make one of his cold, hard demands. When he didn't say a word, I opened my eyes and saw him watching me intently, as if he was waiting to see if I'd obey Kylo like I *sometimes* obeyed him.

"No."

"You have half an hour to waste before your meeting," Kylo said, voice hardening. "Sit."

"No."

Within a moment, Roman moved around the table, grabbed my ass in one hand and my breast in the other, and said, "Either you sit or you spend the next thirty minutes between us with your legs buckling beneath you."

Excitement raced through me. I knew that defying him would make him snap; it always led to him fucking me, and that was what I needed after today even if it was just a quickie. So, I did what I did best and asked, "Is that a vow? Or another one of your lousy, empty promises?"

He ripped me from Kylo's grasp, growled, and bent me over our wooden kitchen table. "Empty promises, Isabella," he spit my words right back at me. "Empty"—he pulled my pants down—"fucking"—he pulled out his cock and slapped it against my wet entrance—"promises." He thrust me against the table. "That's what this is."

I whimpered and arched my back for him.

He snatched a fistful of my hair and pulled me off the table. "Apologize to Kylo."

"Fuck you, Roman."

"Apologize," Roman ordered, his voice so cruel and demeaning. Roman continued to pound into me so hard from behind that my breasts nearly fell out of my bra under my shirt. "Apologize like you would to me. Don't disrespect him."

Kylo seized my chin in one hand and stuck his fingers into my mouth, and then he grabbed my breast in his other hand and rolled the nipple around his palm. I tightened around Roman, a wave of pleasure rushing through me, and reached for Kylo's black jeans.

I stroked his bulge through his pants, gazed up at him, and gagged on his fingers. When he pulled them out of my mouth, he wiped the spit across my cheek.

"Does this make up for it?" I asked, pushing my hand into his pants and stroking him through his briefs. "How about this?"

Roman stilled behind me and tugged harder on my hair. "Does a halfhearted hand job make up for your disrespect?"

My pussy clenched on his cock, and I shook my head. "No."

After pushing me back down onto the table—closer to Kylo's bulge—Roman thrust into me from behind, sending me harder against the wooden edge. I stared at Kylo's bulge through his briefs and pushed my hand under his underwear to grasp his cock in my hand.

I hesitated and glanced back at Roman, who watched me with those demanding golden eyes. I gulped and pulled out Kylo's cock, my mind buzzing, my fingers tingling. This was really happening again.

"Isabella," Raj said through the mind link.

I wanted to ignore him so fucking bad. There was still at least fifteen minutes before our meeting, and I was so close to coming and relaxing for once today. But I couldn't ignore him, not when there was a war in our forest.

"What?" I asked, hoping his response would be quick.

"Scarlett is gone."

CHAPTER 38

ISABELLA

"I thought that you said Scarlett was locked in the fucking cell?" I asked Kylo through clenched teeth as I pulled up and buttoned my pants as quickly as I could and hurried toward the front door.

Stricken with sudden surprise, Kylo redid his jeans and followed me. "She is."

"What's happened?" Roman asked, hurrying after us.

I stormed out the front door in disbelief. This couldn't be happening. I had worked my ass off today at the Lycans' and made no progress. Scarlett had been my only hope at finding Derek alive and getting him through these corrupt times. I should've gone to see her myself before I came home.

What if Kylo *or* Roman had helped her escape?

Kylo was her ex-mate, and Roman had just spent two days with her doing Goddess knew what. She could've hurt one or both of them, mind-controlled them, or promised them something that I would never be able to give them.

Yet I couldn't get myself to believe that either of them was corrupt.

The Moon Goddess had given Kylo and me the responsibility to destroy Dolus. And Roman was my mate, who had loved me since we were just children. They wouldn't betray me. They couldn't.

"Scarlett escaped and killed three guards at the prison," I said, running through the forest.

Roman growled fiercely, shifted into his huge brown wolf, and sprinted ahead of me toward the prison. Kylo and I shifted a couple moments later. Instead of running into the prison with Roman, I ran toward the borders. Scarlett couldn't have gotten far. Someone had helped her escape, and while that someone was good at hiding their tracks, I had people here now who could pick up their scents.

"Get the best trackers we have, Raj," I said through the mind link. Sticking my nose to the ground, I picked up a sweet, feminine scent. *"Raj?"* I asked when he didn't respond. My heart pounded inside my chest as wind whipped around us, blowing my fur in every direction.

"We don't need a tracker ..." Raj finally said, voice a mere whisper in my mind.

"Tell me that you're all right. Tell me that—" I cut the mind link and stopped dead in my tracks.

Standing at our borders, Scarlett had her hand wrapped around the front of a warrior's neck and viciously strummed her claws against her throat. It wasn't just any warrior. It was Vanessa.

I howled, calling for Roman and Kylo to follow me, and sprinted toward a deathly still Raj. Instead of trying to deescalate the situation, Raj gaped at Scarlett with wide, shocked eyes.

Was he ... was he all right?

Scarlett turned toward me with bright, evil eyes and the

same smirk she'd had when she drew her dirty claws against my mate's chest at the Lycans'. "Isabella," she purred. "I'm glad you could make it."

Vanessa grabbed her wrist to yank her away as Scarlett threatened to kill her.

"Put her down," I ordered, voice stern.

Vanessa looked at me with guilt in her wide eyes. She clamped her canines into Scarlett's wrist, and Scarlett actually tensed.

I straightened my back and glared at Scarlett to show her that I wasn't afraid. "Now."

But I was terrified because if I stepped toward her, she'd kill Vanessa, and if I didn't do anything, she'd probably kill her too. We were in a lose-lose type of situation, and nobody was being helpful at the moment.

I glanced back at Raj and followed his stare past Scarlett to … Jane.

Jane stood off to the side as the wind blew her long, pin-straight brown hair into her face. She tucked a strand behind her ear, eyes glazed over and fixed on Scarlett in amazement and pride.

Jane was the mole, not Roman, not Kylo, not Raj, and certainly not Vanessa. *Jane.*

When Roman and Kylo appeared and shifted next to me, Scarlett tossed Vanessa to the side and clapped her hands together. "We're all finally here. No need for you anymore," she said to her.

Vanessa collapsed onto sticks and branches, clutching her neck.

I glanced at her for a moment to make sure she was okay and then growled at Scarlett, "What do you fucking want?" I asked through clenched teeth, feeling nothing but rage. "I should've made them kill you already."

She smirked. "But then I wouldn't get to tell you all the

things that happened between Roman and me the other night." She cackled.

Roman clenched his jaw. "Nothing happened."

I trust Roman. I trust Roman. I trust Roman. I have to trust Roman.

Scarlett stepped forward and tilted her head. "Are you sure about that, Romie?"

I moved between the two of them and focused all my attention on that lying, man-stealing piece of shit. "I'm not going to fall for your stupid mind games. You didn't—" I stopped short when she pushed some hair off of her shoulder and showed me her freshly marked and blistering neck.

No. No. No. No. No. No. No.

Scarlett was just playing a game with me. Another fucking game.

It wasn't real.

Roman hadn't marked her.

Pushing all my fears to the side, I stepped closer to her, clenched my jaw, and really looked at it. Everything else seemed to blur. And all my wolf could focus on were the large canine marks and the disgusting arrogance radiating off of her.

Though the mark was almost alpha-sized, the canine marks weren't as big as Roman's. I knew firsthand. I had stared at my mark for hours after Roman claimed me; I knew how they looked. He hadn't marked her, which meant that—

I glanced over at Kylo, feeling heartbroken. "Did you—"

Before I could finish the sentence, Kylo flashed me his canines, which were just as big as Roman's. No, he hadn't bitten her either. I furrowed my brows and stepped away from Scarlett, everything seeming to click in my head.

This was a setup. She had something planned.

"Whoever is near Roman's pack, I need you at the west border now," I said through the mind link to my Lycans. Something

was about to go terribly wrong. I could just feel it. *"Doctors, trackers, warriors."*

Nobody moved. Deafening silence fell over the forest. Dolus was here.

"Roman didn't mark you," I said to Scarlett, trying to buy time for my warriors to get here. If Dolus had taken down the Moon Goddess, then two alphas, two Lycans, and a warrior wouldn't be able to defeat him alone. "You're a liar."

"Wow," she said. "You're really good at picking up on things, aren't you?"

"Who marked you?" I asked, pushing Roman and Kylo back a few feet. *"Go protect the—"*

"She-she did it," Raj said, his voice a mere whisper as he pointed at Jane.

My heart dropped at how Raj must've felt, knowing that his mate—the one woman he was supposed to love for eternity—had marked someone else.

Jane sneered at Raj and stepped forward. "I did mark her."

"You marked Scarlett?" Roman roared, his mind link buzzing with vengeance and fury and every curse word in the damn book. *"You* were the one working with Scarlett? You helped her escape? You kidnapped Derek?"

"Derek?" I whispered, thrusting a hand to my chest. I looked around for him, hoping that they had been dumb enough to bring him back here and hide him behind some blowing tree branches. "Where is he?"

Jane took a threatening step toward me, her hands clasped behind her back and her lifeless, almost-hazy eyes narrowed at me. "It doesn't matter where he is. All you have to know is that he's not coming back for you. Nobody is."

It took everything I had in me not to lunge at her and kill her. She was being controlled by Dolus. This wasn't the Jane that I had grown up with, this wasn't the Jane who loved

Vanessa, this wasn't the Jane who annoyed Roman every chance she got.

"Jane," Raj said. He moved his lips more, but no words came out. His chin trembled, yet all he could do was stare at her. His mate had marked someone else. It had to hurt worse than the heat I had gone through without Roman.

She slowly approached me and stopped a foot away from me, her dreary green eyes darkening by the second. I stood my ground and refused to look at her or back away from her. If Dolus had taken control of her, if he were inside of her, he had another thing coming. I wouldn't be intimidated by Roman's sister.

"Jane," Roman said, voice barely above a whisper. Though he tried to show no signs of being intimidated, I could feel just how badly he hurt on the inside. We were connected and shared emotions like no other, and his were agonizingly painful right now. "No, this can't be happening. I can't lose you too. Mom and Dad and now … now you."

My heart clenched. Roman had already been through a world full of pain. Now that his sister had been taken by Dolus, I didn't know if he would ever recover from something this devastating. This would be the first step to Dolus controlling his mind.

"Isabella needs to go," Scarlett said to Jane, canines glistening with thick yellowish saliva. "We can't rule the world with her in this pack and in this world. She's the only thing standing in our way of domination."

Jane's eyes trembled, switching between dull greens to her bright emerald color for a mere moment. Then, Scarlett snapped her fingers, and everything from there happened in a complete blur.

Raj shrieked. Vanessa sprinted toward me. And Jane pulled a silver dagger from behind her back, aimed it at me, and slashed it through the air. Just as the knife was about to pierce my skin, Vanessa shoved me away. The blade slid right through the center of her chest, cutting through her sternum like a hot knife in butter.

"We need a doctor," I screamed through the mind link as I scrambled to my knees and pressed my hands against Vanessa's wound, so she wouldn't bleed out. Tears streamed down my cheeks. *"We need a doctor now."*

This was all my fault.

"Why?" I shouted at Jane through the tears. "Why would you do this?"

Jane dropped the knife, letting it impale the muddy forest floor. Under the moonlight, her face contorted back and forth between stunned, surprised, and shocked, her eyes shifting through a hundred shades of gold, as if she was struggling with something inside of her—a beast who wanted to be free.

"Vanessa!" Jane shouted.

Roman growled at Scarlett, teeth lengthening into canines. "What the fuck did you do to her?"

Scarlett wrapped her arms around Jane's shoulders and pulled Jane in front of her like the fucking wimp she was, using people as fucking shields to stay alive. Whether *she was* Dolus or still Scarlett, she had always been and always would be a weak piece of shit.

"I need a doctor now. Someone, please," I pleaded through the mind link.

But nobody was responding.

Kylo scooped Vanessa up into his arms. "I'll take her to the hospital."

"Make sure she gets to my mom," I said. "And come back quickly, please, Kylo. We're going to need you."

After he sprinted through the forest toward the hospital, I turned back around to see Scarlett sneering at my Roman, her red lips in a cruel smirk.

"Don't want me to hurt your precious sister, do you?" She let out a bone-chilling laugh. "I know how much she means to you ... but she's already gone, Romie." Scarlett grazed her knuckles against Jane's cheek.

Like a cat would with their owner, Jane closed her eyes and brushed her head against Scarlett's neck. "Yes, mate," she said as if she had been mind-controlled and completely forgotten about what she had just done to Vanessa—her best friend.

Raj roared beside me and lunged at Scarlett, but I grabbed his wrist and yanked him back. Scarlett wanted us to fight. She wanted us to break, physically and mentally, so she could bring us down. She was working with Dolus ... or maybe, just maybe, she was Dolus herself.

"Jane," I said her name softly and stepped forward. Dark clouds moved overhead, blocking any sort of sun or moonlight. "Do you really want to kill your luna?" I asked, watching her brow jerk. "Do you want to kill your brother's mate? Do you know how devastated he would be to know that the only family he had left killed his own mate?" I continued.

Jane's lip twitched again, but talking to her about her family and friends wasn't enough to get her to snap out of the trance.

Scarlett whispered something in her ear.

I stepped closer to her, eyes locked on to Jane's. "Do you know what your mate would do if you killed his partner and the leader of the Lycans?" I asked. "The woman who saved you and him from that vicious man we once called Ryker?"

"He would break," Scarlett said, stroking her hair and smiling down at her. "Just like we want him to break. You'll be doing good work, Jane."

Tears welled up in Jane's dull eyes. She parted her lips to

speak but couldn't say anything. She moved them some more but didn't utter a single word, only some small gasps.

Roman furrowed his brows at her. "What do you want, Jane? Anything."

Her skin flushed a deep red. My words had seemed to hit her right in the heart. And while I didn't want to hurt her, she needed to pull herself out of the trance that Scarlett had put her in. Hurting her might be the only way.

"Your mate would reject you," I said, stepping forward. "Your brother would disown you. All of your friends would hate you for it. You would have nobody left. Not your parents. Not your brother. Not your mate. You'd become a lone wolf and have to fend for yourself, with nobody to see or talk to, except yourself."

When Jane let out a piercing, pain-filled scream, Scarlett said some more of her sorcery shit under her breath. Jane began to seize back and forth, foam filling her mouth and leaking down her chin. Suddenly, charcoal darkness permeated through the whites of Scarlett's eyes.

"You've served me well, Jane," Scarlett said, voice as deep as a man. "Thank you, child."

As Scarlett stepped away from Jane, Jane stopped seizing and collapsed onto the ground.

Before she could smash her head in, Roman caught her in his arms and started muttering, *"No,"* over and over again.

Raj snatched her from Roman, held her to his chest, and pushed a hand through her chocolate-brown hair. "Baby, no. Come back to me. Come back. Snap out of it, Jane," he pleaded, voice cracking.

From afar, I could hear the steady beat of Jane's heart, but she was unresponsive.

Scarlett had done something to her, something evil.

Jane snapped her arm out and wrapped her hand around Raj's neck, eyes completely black.

Raj collapsed on the ground, holding his neck. "Jane," he whispered. "Jane, please. It's me, your mate."

"I have no mate," Jane said. "Except Scarlett."

"Please, Moon Goddess, help us," I begged, knowing that it wouldn't be any use.

Scarlett chuckled deeply. "The Moon Goddess is gone. I locked her away. She will never return."

It was official. Kylo and I were the only ones who could save our species now.

CHAPTER 39

ISABELLA

*T*he Moon Goddess had been defeated. The woman we had worshipped for centuries was trapped in corruption until we could help her escape. Her power hadn't been strong enough to keep Dolus away, and I didn't know if *anything* would be powerful enough to defeat him.

Would mates still form? Had the Moon Goddess given us the power to choose our mates when she left this world? What would happen during full moons? Would my moon-flowers on my windowsill still glow for her deep into the night?

I didn't know, and it terrified me.

Dolus now stood in front of me as Scarlett and smirked.

I stared right into Scarlett's black eyes and bared my teeth at her. "I'm not afraid of you, Dolus. I am building an army to destroy you. Tearing down one person isn't going to tear down us all. Together, we're strong enough to defeat you."

Scarlett smiled a bit too sweetly at me as someone ran

through the woods to our west. For a moment, I thought it was Kylo coming back to help me end this once and for all, but Derek emerged from the woods, breathing hard.

My eyes widened, warmth filling my body. "Derek, it's you. You're okay."

Derek shifted into his human form and smiled at me, showing me his pearly-white teeth. "Isabella," Derek said, almost as if nothing had ever happened to him.

He walked closer to us, standing between Scarlett and me. All I wanted to do was wrap my arms around his body and pull him close.

Yet when I stepped toward him, Kylo—who must've gotten back from the hospital—caught my wrist and pulled me back, his gaze focused on Scarlett. "What're you doing?" he asked me.

"Derek," I said, pointing toward him.

Derek's smile widened even more. "Izzy."

"There isn't anyone here, Isabella," Kylo said, grip on me tightening as he pulled me closer to his chest. "She's showing you things that aren't there. She's in your head. Don't let her stay."

"But …" I shook my head. *Derek was really here.* "He's here. He's right here."

"No," Kylo said against me, "he's not."

My stomach tightened as a lump formed in my throat. I pressed my lips together and stared at Derek, but …

What if it's all in my mind? What if she had already corrupted me in the mere few moments that she had been here?

I looked back at Scarlett. "Where is Derek?"

"He's right here," she said, pointing toward Derek, who had his arms outstretched for me to hug him.

Goddess, I wanted to touch him so bad. I didn't want him to still be gone, out there in the wild for so long.

"Why don't you give him a hug? It'll prove it to you."

"Where is he? What are you doing to him? Where have you taken him?" I asked, tearing my gaze away and refusing to believe that he was here in front of me.

While I saw him, Kylo didn't. And if Kylo didn't see him too … it must all be in my head.

Scarlett smirked and glanced at Derek, whose smile turned into one of pain.

He sat in a dark prison cell, his body completely naked and covered with open scars spewing blood. He gazed at me with tears in his eyes. "Izzy! Izzy, please help me. She's … she's hurting me, and I can't stop it. I'm not strong enough. I'm weak. I'm so weak," he said, voice broken.

Seeing Derek so defeated, I lunged at Scarlett again and was pulled back by Kylo. If only just a bit, Kylo's touch calmed me enough to think clearer while my mind was foggy with hate and rage.

To my left, Roman ripped Jane off of Raj, who had deep puncture wounds in his neck. Jane flailed her arms and legs as Roman held her tighter and tighter, trapping her arms so she couldn't break free. She let out another piercing scream.

When Scarlett said, "That's enough," to her, Jane stopped immediately and fell limp in Roman's arms.

I gulped. Dolus had more power than I'd thought.

But why wasn't he attacking us directly? What was stopping him from inflicting physical damage? Why did he have to use Jane and Derek to hurt us? Something wasn't fucking right, and I didn't want to wait for him to make his next move.

"If you want to hurt me, then hurt me, but leave my friends alone," I said.

To my surprise, Dolus lunged at me. I dodged out of the way of his first attack, closed my eyes for a single moment, and opened them up to see a hundred Scarletts around the woods, all sprinting in my direction.

My gaze flickered to each one. Everything was happening so quickly that I couldn't pick out who was who or which one was the real Scarlett. And when I looked back at my friends, they all turned into her too.

Roman was Scarlett.

Jane was Scarlett.

Raj was Scarlett.

Kylo was Scarlett.

I was alone, so terribly alone.

"Roman," I called out, bracing myself for impact.

One of them was going to attack me and hit me, bring me to the ground and kill me if I wasn't careful. I squeezed my eyes shut and then reopened them, hoping that they would disappear. Yet when I opened my eyes, they were even closer.

Someone stuck me hard from behind, and I smacked against the ground with a thud. Rocks cut into my palms and split open my knees. I stumbled up to my feet and turned around to see ten of her stalking toward me.

My lips quivered. Dolus was fucking with my mind. He was inside of it, trying to get me to break.

One leaped at me, shoved me to the ground, and hopped over me, attacking a Scarlett from behind me. I dug my nails into the dirt and pushed myself back up.

Goddess, what was I going to do? I couldn't tell who was who.

There were three others fighting in front of me, who I assumed were Jane, Raj, and my Roman. I took a deep breath, trying to focus on the ground.

"Someone," I said through the mind link, hoping to contact a warrior from the Lycans.

Yet nobody responded.

We were going to die here. We were all going to fucking die.

But I wouldn't die without a fight.

My nails lengthened into sharp claws, my teeth hungry canines. I shifted into my wolf and charged at all the Scarletts. When I collided with one, I sprinted right through her, and she disappeared into thin air.

They were penetrable.

So, I continued to run toward each one, bracing myself for impact but never hitting anything. Most of them disappeared into thin air while some of the stronger ones lingered in the forest. I gazed around for my next victim when someone hit me from behind and knocked me down.

I flew forward and smacked against a tree trunk, branches stabbing into my underbelly. From the intense pain, my wolf forced me to shift into my human form. I grasped my elbow, trying to pop it back into place before she could attack me again, but she hit me straight in the spine.

Doubling over into the dirt, I posted my palms on the ground to try to stand, but she was really fucking strong. I used all my strength to turn onto my back and stared right up at her. But it wasn't Scarlett; it was Derek again—at least, an image of him.

"Do it," I spit at him through clenched teeth. "Try to kill me."

He wrapped his hands around my neck and squeezed. "Roman and Kylo will choose me once this is all over. I'm going to break them. I'm going to make them suffer because of you, whore."

Someone shouted toward the east, and then Derek was shoved off me and tackled to the ground, a silver knife sliding through the back of his throat. Naomi stood over Derek, a bead of sweat rolling down her forehead. I grasped her arm. All the other Scarletts disappeared, and the seven of us were left in the woods together.

As if the silver knife had had no effect on him, Derek

stood up and pulled it out. "We'll meet again, Isabella." He hurled the knife right back at us.

I pulled Naomi to the ground as it whizzed right over her head and hit a tree. When I looked back up, Scarlett was gone, and the real Derek sat against a tree, clutching his broken ribs and open wounds.

"Get Jane," Kylo said from beside me to Roman as he scooped me up into his arms. "I got Isabella."

When they started walking toward the hospital, I scrambled up into Kylo's arms and stared back at Derek, who still sat in the middle of the forest, frowning at me and begging me to come get him.

Tears welled up in my eyes, and I frowned. He wasn't real, just a figment of my imagination. Fake. Made up. Not really there. Not really breathing. Not really real ... but he looked so real and so hurt.

Kylo held me tighter, so I wouldn't scurry out of his hold and run toward nothingness. I wrapped my arms around Kylo's neck and continued to stare back at Derek until I couldn't see him anymore. I squeezed my eyes closed, my nails digging into Kylo's back.

"I'm coming for you, Derek. Stay strong," I said through the mind link, though I knew he couldn't hear me.

Tears streamed down my face.

For the first time in my entire life, I felt helpless. I had two mates by my side, I was stronger than I ever had been, and I had led the Lycans to victory time and time again, but I couldn't destroy Dolus as easily as I'd thought I'd be able to.

Kylo opened the hospital door and walked into the building. Doctors scrambled around the waiting room, ushering us to rooms to be checked out. They had probably expected a bloodbath and open wounds, cuts that wouldn't heal for months upon months, but what they got was much worse.

Roman was grasping an unresponsive Jane in his arms, holding her tight to his chest, whispering that this would all be okay. Tears flowed down his cheeks, his lips quivering. He was yelling for someone to help his sister ... but nobody knew how to help her. What could they do to someone who had been attacked by a demonic god's magic?

Dad pulled Jane out of Roman's arms and told him that they would try their best to help her. As he carried Jane, he hurried to one of the back rooms, followed by Mom and a flock of nurses and doctors. I stared at the busy, bland hallways and almost broke down into tears, but I held my shit together because Roman and Raj were too far gone emotionally for me to be a mess too.

"Please ... watch Roman," I said to Kylo. "I have to go check on Vanessa."

"Wait." Kylo grasped my hand and pulled me back to him. "Are you okay?" Brows furrowed together, he stepped closer to me and tucked some hair behind my ear. "Dolus targeted you with that last attack. I want to make sure that you're good. Everyone needs you, Isabella, even me."

"I'm okay," I whispered, but my voice wavered.

Everything had happened so fast; I barely had time to register it. All I could think about were my friends and how they might die or be corrupted because of me. If I had actually believed it was Derek and run into his arms, everyone might've died.

I glanced back up at him through tears. "If I'm not, I'll tell you and Roman. I promise."

After a few calm moments amid the chaos, Kylo released my hand. I shakily walked down the hall and looked in each room for Vanessa.

Rachel—the woman I used to work with—gave me a half-smile from the counter. "Vanessa?" She nodded toward the stairs. "Room 506."

Once I made it to Room 506, I stopped in front of Vanessa's open door. In a bed with her eyes closed and a ventilator attached to her mouth, Vanessa lay so still with her blonde hair pushed to one side, chest patched up with some gauze.

"Vanessa," I whispered. My fingers trembled when I reached for her hand. "Vanessa, I'm so sorry." I slid into the bed with her, resting my head on her shoulder and wrapping my arm around her stomach, like she did to me whenever I slept over at her house.

Fat, ugly tears streamed down my face. I bit my lip to hold back my cries, but I couldn't. My body heaved back and forth on the bed next to her.

"Everything is going to be okay," I said to her as I brushed some hair out of her face. "Everything will be great." But I was saying it more for myself than I was for her. I needed something to believe in, and as crazy as it was, Vanessa gave me hope.

Someone who had once made my life hell had given me so much hope.

For fifteen minutes, I sobbed in her bed and stared up at the dry and drab ceiling. "Thank you for everything that you've done for this pack." I stood up and brushed another strand of her hair out of her face. "I don't know if I'll ever get the chance to see you again, but I wanted to say thank you." I leaned over her and pressed my lips to her cheek. Her heart monitor skipped a beat, and I actually smiled. "You haven't gone unnoticed."

Then, I walked out of her room and back down the stairs to meet Roman, who had calmed down, and Kylo, who stood next to him, gripping his shoulder.

I walked right past them, grabbing them by the hands, and toward my office. "Come on. We have a Moon Goddess to save and a god to kill."

. . .

Continued in Protecting the Alpha.

ALSO BY EMILIA ROSE

Order the final installment of the Submission Trilogy now:
Protecting the Alpha

Some other books written by Emilia Rose

Come Here, Kitten

Catch Me, Alpha

Alpha Maddox

ABOUT THE AUTHOR

Emilia Rose is an international bestselling author of steamy paranormal romance. With over 3,000 monthly subscribers on Patreon and over 15 million story views online, Emilia loves creating the newest and sexiest paranormal romances for her fans.

Sign up for her newsletter to receive the latest news, goodies, and giveaways right in your inbox! Sign up HERE

Printed in Great Britain
by Amazon